46519

Books by Matt Christopher

Sports Stories

Animal Stories

THE
TWENTY-ONE-
MILE
SWIM

THE TWENTY-ONE-MILE SWIM

by Matt Christopher

Little, Brown and Company

BOSTON   **TORONTO**

FIRST EDITION

Library of Congress Cataloging in Publication Data

Christopher, Matthew F
  The twenty-one-mile swim.

  SUMMARY: With remarks about his small stature and
poor swimming skills ringing in his ears, the son of
Hungarian immigrants begins to train for the 21-mile
swim across a nearby lake.
  [1. Swimming—Fiction. 2. Identity—Fiction.
3. Hungarian American—Fiction] I. Title.
PZ7.C458Tv [Fic]   79–15197
ISBN 0–316–13979–3

BP

*Published simultaneously in Canada
by Little, Brown & Company (Canada) Limited*

PRINTED IN THE UNITED STATES OF AMERICA

To Cora and Gus

THE
TWENTY-ONE-
MILE
SWIM

THE FIRST YEAR

1

"HI, PEEWEE! Want a ride?"

Joey Vass looked up. He was standing on the end of the twenty-foot long, three-foot wide dock that projected out into the lake, watching small fish swimming around in the shallow water beneath him. He was fourteen, five-foot three inches tall and weighed a hundred and twenty-one pounds. But he wasn't amused by anybody's calling him Peewee.

"In that little boat?" he shouted back to the caller.

Ross Cato laughed. "No! In that big boat!" he answered, letting go of the right-hand oar of the rowboat to point at the sailboat moored to a buoy some sixty feet off shore. Sitting at the stern was

3

Paula Kantella, her long blond hair whipping about her pretty face.

"How long you going to be gone?" Joey asked.

"About an hour! Come on!"

Joey thought about it.

"It's a lot of fun if you've never been on a sailboat before!" Ross said.

Joey had never been on a sailboat in his life.

A grin spread across his oval face. "I haven't got trunks!" he said.

"That's okay! Come on, anyway!" replied Ross, and started to row the boat toward shore in Joey's direction. With Paula's weight holding down the stern, the bow of the ten-foot, wooden rowboat glided up on the graveled shore with a protesting crunch and ground to a stop.

"Just give it a little shove and hop in," advised Ross.

Joey did so, getting his sneakers wet in the process. The boat slid out, and Ross began to row with short, jerky turns of the oars. After they reached deeper water, he turned the boat around with expertise and started to row to the sailboat.

"Did you ever ride on a sailboat?" Ross asked, taking long, even strokes now that shot the boat across the water in swift, even strides. He was wearing red trunks and a red band around his forehead. His back and shoulder muscles bulged like rope on his six-foot, streamlined frame. He had the sleek physique of a swimmer, developed over the past few years doing laps in the pool at Merton High.

"Never," said Joey.

"Always been a landlubber?"

"Right."

"How come you moved near a lake?"

"My father always wanted to live by water," explained Joey. "He likes to fish, and he likes boats. So, here we are."

He caught Paula's green eyes looking at him over Ross's gleaming shoulder. She had on a white two-piece swimsuit and held a white rubber cap on her lap. "My dad loves fishing, too," she said. "And he knows some good spots. Bass, trout — fish like that. They ought to get together sometime."

"Good idea," said Joey.

On the other hand, he wasn't sure that they would. Both his mother and father were immigrants. They had come to the United States from Hungary when the communists took over the country. Even though that had happened more than twenty years ago, their English vocabulary was still limited, and their speech was noticeably accented. They were usually self-conscious and reluctant to make new acquaintances.

They neared the sailboat, and Ross said, "Grab the line, Joey."

Joey grabbed the line; at the end of it was a snap-on latch hooked to a round metal loop secured to a buoy. Ross laid the oars inside the rowboat, hooked the rowboat's line to the loop, and took the line from Joey.

"Okay. Hop in," he said as they pulled the rowboat alongside the sailboat.

It was a twenty-one foot, fiberglass cabin model, a streamlined beauty whose smooth, white hull glistened in the bright June sunlight. A burst of admiration went through Joey as he began to realize that his dream of riding on the boat was coming true. He had first seen the sailboat when it was brought here about the middle of May. Twice it had gone out with two people aboard, one of whom, Joey now realized, was Ross. The other was an older man, probably Ross's father. The tall, triangular sails billowing out before the wind and the boat sailing through the water, bent slightly by the wind, had been a picture he had hoped to be a part of someday. Now, today, the time had unexpectedly come.

"Loosen up those halyards, Joey," said Ross, pointing at the sail tied around the boom.

Halyards? Is he pulling my leg by using sailing lingo on me? Joey wondered.

"I'll help you," offered Paula.

While they worked to free the sail, Ross got the tiller out of the hold and secured it in position.

"Hey, man, if you got up off your knees you could work faster," he said to Joey.

Joey, unraveling the sail from the boom, shrugged, and smiled to show that the wisecrack didn't bother him — even though it did. He wondered why Ross had asked him to join them. Was it just to look better than him and show off to Paula? "We can't all be tall Adonises like you, Ross," he said.

"Right," said Paula. "Everybody can't be a six-footer like you are."

"Six and one-half inch, to be exact," said Ross, straightening up his solid, sun-browned frame.

"Ugh," snorted Paula. "Talk about modesty."

He laughed. "Okay, let's quit the chatter and get these rags hoisted," he said seriously. "Paula, grab the tiller, will you?"

Joey met Paula's eyes and saw them look skyward in an expression that clearly indicated she didn't think much of Ross's self-adoration.

He didn't know how the two knew each other since they went to different schools. Ross was sixteen, a junior at Merton High. Paula was fourteen, a student at Gatewood Central, and Joey's height. But he didn't need glasses to see why Ross could be attracted to Paula. She was the prettiest girl he had seen since his family had moved here.

She sat on the stern seat and grabbed the tiller while Ross raised the jib and then the mainsail. The boat was already starting to move through the water, drawn by the wind as it filled the sails. Ross secured all the lines; then he went and took over control of the tiller from Paula.

"You two put on life jackets," he ordered. "They're right behind you, Shorty."

Joey found the bright orange life jackets and tossed one to Paula. He watched her put it over her head so that it rested against her neck and shoulders and began to do likewise with his. He pulled the cloth belt tight around his chest and knotted it, just as a gust of wind hit the sails, tipping the boat enough to knock him off balance and almost into the water. He sat down hard, grabbing the side of the boat in a vise-like grip.

"Sorry about that, Joey," said Ross. "These

gusts come up without warning sometimes. Hey, you're not scared, are you? Your face is white as that sail. You okay?"

"Yeah, I'm okay."

He was now, but a moment ago he wasn't. The fear of being thrown into the water had struck him like an ice-cold shower, for he hardly knew how to swim. Not until now, when he had his wits gathered together again, did he realize that his life jacket would have kept him afloat.

"You can swim, can't you?" said Paula, her wide green eyes centered on him.

He forced a grin. "Not — not very well," he confessed.

"Joey! You're kidding!"

"No, I'm not. I've never swum very much in my life."

"And you live by a lake?" exclaimed Ross. "I can't believe it."

"I told you why we moved here," Joey replied, trying to ignore Ross's tone of voice. "It was my father's idea. Anyway, swimming is going to be the first thing I'm going to learn to do well."

Suddenly he wished he had refused Ross's invitation to go sailing. Joey hadn't expected anything more than a nice ride. Instead, his close call had turned up the embarrassing fact that he was a very poor swimmer.

"Too bad you're not going to Merton," said Ross. "Coach Harvey would have you swimming fine in nothing flat."

"I bet," said Joey.

"He would," insisted Ross, the wind whipping at his brown, curly hair. "He's the best around. The only thing is, though, you'd never make it as a sprinter."

Joey looked at him. "Why not?"

"You're too short. Our shortest sprinter is six inches taller than you."

"What has size got to do with it?" Paula cut in, her tone edgy.

"A lot," said Ross. "How many little guys do you know in our school who have won meets? Including kids in the middle grades?"

Joey's neck reddened. He could tolerate the "little guys" bit, but he hated to be told that he couldn't do something just because he was short.

"I couldn't go to Merton if I wanted to," he said, trying hard to keep his emotions under control. "It's not in our district."

"Well, if you did you might do all right against those seventh and eighth graders," said Ross. "Most of them are about your size."

"Ross! What nerve!" exclaimed Paula hotly. "How can you sit there and talk to Joey like that? Just because he's shorter than a lot of boys his age doesn't mean that he can't be a strong competitor! I think you owe him an apology!"

"Oh, cool it, Paula," said Ross tersely. "I didn't say anything to him that I have to apologize for. Did I, Joey? Look, if you think I did —"

"Forget it," said Joey. "We came out for a ride, not a debate."

"Right." Ross smiled and shot a glance at Paula as if to see if Joey's comment satisfied her.

He could see it didn't.

"Okay," said Ross. "If it makes you feel better, I apologize. Women! Always raising a stink about the puniest thing."

He turned the tiller slightly, maneuvering the boat so that it leaned harder into the wind. The move was almost as if he had done it purposely, a blunt act of irritation.

"What did you say?" Paula said, frowning at him. Then she turned her face into the wind so that it caught her blond hair and flung it furiously around her head. "Oh, never mind," she said, her words swallowed up by the wind.

They sailed to the opposite side of the lake,

11

then came about and sailed northward. Joey, temporarily forgetting Ross's references to his small stature, was impressed by Ross's seamanship. Maybe the guy was stuck on himself for being a good swimmer, but he certainly knew how to handle a sailboat.

2

AFTER almost forty-five minutes of tacking back and forth, running first a northerly course and then a southerly, Ross headed the sailboat home. He maneuvered it into a position so that the sails lost the wind and went limp as it approached the buoy, drawing up close enough to it so that Joey was able to hook the line to it.

"Attaboy, Joey," Ross said amiably. "You've got the makings of a sailor — at least."

He glanced at Paula as he spoke, a mischievous glint in his eyes, and Joey knew that Ross had added the last two words to tease her.

She offered no comment but took off her life jacket, which reminded Joey that he had his to remove, too.

After the sails were lowered and fastened to the boom, the three got into the rowboat, and Ross rowed Joey to shore.

"Thanks for the ride," said Joey, hopping out. "See you again, maybe."

"Maybe by the next time you'll have learned to swim better and won't worry about falling out of a boat," remarked Ross.

"Maybe," said Joey.

He gave the boat a shove away from shore, and Ross took it from there, applying his oars in short, rapid motions that propelled the little vessel along the shoreline northward toward Paula's cottage. Actually, the cottage was both a winter and summer home for her and her parents ever since they had moved here some eight years ago.

Coming down the wooden steps to the red deck was a contingent to greet him: his two sisters, Yolanda and Mary, and the youngest member of the Vass clan, his brother Gabor. Yolanda was sixteen, the eldest of the lot; Mary was eleven and Gabor eight. At five feet three and a quarter inch, Yolanda was exactly half an inch taller than Joey. He often thought that at the slow rate he was growing, that half-inch might as well be a foot.

"Well!" exclaimed Yolanda, wisps of her dark hair blowing across her face. "The sailor's back. How'd you rate a ride on Mr. Cato's sailboat, anyway?"

"I have a hunch that Paula had something to do with it," admitted Joey.

"Oh," chimed in Mary, "you admit that." Her black hair was cut shorter than her sister's mainly because it could pack up easier under her softball cap when she played.

Joey, grinning, made a motion as if to cuff her across the ear. She ducked away from him, laughing.

"I'd like a ride on that sailboat sometime," said Gabor, staring off dreamily at the boat lying anchored in the distance. "Suppose Ross would take me, Joey?"

"Isn't Ross a bit older than Paula?" Yolanda asked Joey, totally ignoring her younger brother.

"Why?" spoke up Mary. "Any particular reason why you'd like to know?"

"I'm talking!" piped up Gabor irritably, his small voice suddenly loud enough to suppress the other voices around him.

Joey looked at him, smiling. "I heard you, Gabe," he said. "And the answer is, I don't know. Maybe he will, and maybe he won't."

Gabor stared at him with his soft blue eyes. "What do you mean?"

Joey shrugged. "Just that. Maybe he will, and maybe he won't. I don't know him well enough yet to ask him if he will."

"Maybe Daddy will buy a sailboat," he said, his eyes suddenly shining as he looked at the sailboat.

"I don't know about that," said Joey. "Dad's interested in fishing, and fishermen don't go for sailboats."

"Is Ross still in school?" asked Yolanda. "He looks about nineteen or twenty to me."

"He's in the eleventh grade, I think," said Joey. "Which makes him about sixteen or seventeen."

"He's real tall, isn't he?"

Joey tried to ignore that comment from Mary, even though he didn't think she had said it to tease him.

"I smell smoke, Mary," said Yolanda cautiously. "I don't think your brother is interested in any further discussion about Ross Cato."

Mary giggled.

Joey, halfway up the steps, stopped abruptly and gave his sisters a cold stare. He started to say something, but changed his mind and ran up the remaining few steps. He'd be darned if he was going to let Ross Cato's name bother him.

He headed across the immaculate green lawn toward the white, wood-shingled house. The house was fronted by a windowed porch covered with venetian blinds to use when the sun became unbearably hot.

Instead of entering by the front door, however, he went around to the back door and entered into the narrow foyer and then into the small kitchen. Everything looked spic and span. He loved his mother's tidiness. Maybe she wasn't well educated and spoke English with an accent, he thought, but she was tops in house cleaning and a darned good cook, too.

He saw from a quick glance at the electric clock above the sink that it was almost two-thirty. He started into the living room, smelling the familiar odor of fresh tobacco smoke, when he heard footsteps and met his father coming toward him.

"Well, hi, Joey," his father greeted him, taking a curve-stemmed pipe out of his mouth. "We watched you ride on that sailboat. It looked like a lot of fun."

"It was," said Joey.

His father backed into the living room, and

Joey followed him. He was slightly taller than Joey, but heavier. His hair was brown, cut short. "Come in here. Your mother and I have come to a decision."

Joey saw his mother sitting in an armchair, working on needlepoint. She glanced up at him, her round face breaking into a smile.

"Yes, sure," she said. "We have come to a decision. Ha-ha! He means he has. I just approved." She pronounced "we" as "ve."

"Okay, I'll bite," said Joey, smiling. "What's Dad decided that you approved?"

"He wants to buy a boat," said his mother. "You know that. For weeks he has been talking about it."

"Yes, but —"

"I saw an advertisement in this morning's paper," interrupted his father. "The boat is for sale for seventy-five dollars."

"Seventy-five dollars?" Joey echoed. "It can't be too big at that price."

"It's big enough for what I want," said his father. "It's ten feet long. The oars are included in the price."

Joey smiled. The boat was less than half the length of Ross Cato's sailboat. But, as his father had said, it was big enough for what he wanted.

"Have you called the person?"

"Yes. I said I'd be coming over sometime this afternoon to see it."

"Okay. Let's go."

They drove to the opposite side of the lake where the seller of the rowboat lived in a small home with a dock leading some fifteen feet out into the water. A sixteen-foot Chris Craft outboard, resting in a hoist near it, captured Joey's eye.

"That's what we ought to have, Dad," he said.

"Maybe someday," said his father, hopefully. "Today, though, we'll settle for a little rowboat."

It was an old one. How old Joey couldn't guess. But the paint on it was peeling and the sides were rough from a lot of use.

"I'm sorry," said his father to the man selling the boat. "It looks pretty old. I don't think it's worth seventy-five dollars."

"How about seventy?"

"Make it sixty," said Joey's father.

"You play a hard bargain," said the man. He was tall, gnarled looking, and in his sixties.

"Take it or leave it," said Joey's father with finality.

"Okay, I'll take it," the man said drily.

"Thank you," said Joey's father and wrote out a check.

They were able to tie the boat on the roof of the car, and then they drove home and parked alongside a gray two-door Ford parked in the driveway.

"Aunt Liza's here," observed Joey.

"I see," said his father. "And I can already tell you almost everything she has told your mother about my buying a boat."

"Why? Doesn't she like boats?"

"She likes nothing to do with water," said his father, turning off the ignition. "Ever since her boy Janos drowned, just thinking about water scares her to death."

Joey wondered what she would have thought if she had seen him riding in the sailboat, especially during those moments when it had heeled at such a precarious angle that it seemed it might tip over.

They got out of the car as the other children came running out of the house. Joey and his father took the boat off the roof and, with the other children's help, carried it down to the lake.

"Where you going to keep it, Daddy?" asked Gabor.

"When it's not in use, on shore. Right here, far enough from the water so that the waves will not get to it and maybe work the boat down into the lake. Anyway, it will be tied so it won't get away."

Gabor put an arm around his father's waist and hugged him. Then his father picked him up, and Gabor gave him a kiss on his cheeks.

"I love you, Daddy," he said.

"And I love you, Gabor," said his father.

"Oh, boy," said Joey, grinning. "You know what *that* was for, don't you?"

They returned to the house and found Aunt Liza's reception just as lukewarm as Joey expected it to be. She was his father's sister, a dark-haired, plump woman in her early forties, who, like her brother, had been born in Hungary and immigrated to the United States before she was in her teens.

"You must be crazy, Gabor," she exclaimed, talking to him in Hungarian. "After what happened to Janos, I thought you would think twice before you bought this place by the lake. Now you go and purchase a boat. Wasn't Janos's drowning lesson enough?"

"Accidents can happen no matter what you do," Joey's father replied tersely.

"But you need not put yourself in a place

where you know it could unexpectedly happen," she came back at him. "Janos was a good swimmer, yet he —"

"Enough, Liza," her brother cut in sharply. "I like to fish, and I like to fish from a boat. I won't be swimming while I fish."

Joey, understanding the language better than he could speak it, sympathized with his aunt, although he could not agree entirely with her. What's more, what was done was done, and trying to change his father's mind now was like trying to change the course of the sun.

Aunt Liza made some comment in Hungarian that Joey didn't catch. But apparently his father did, for a grin suddenly laced his face as he said, "That's not nice, Liza."

Both Liza and Joey's mother laughed, easing the situation somewhat. Sometimes he wondered about some of the words that they deliberately said in such a way that they were difficult to hear. Perhaps they did it purposely so that certain ears couldn't catch what they were.

It wasn't until noon on Monday that Joey saw Paula long enough to talk to. They sat in the school cafeteria, and they lingered over their lunch.

"Thought any more about learning to swim better?" Paula asked.

She was wearing a blue jumpsuit which, Joey thought, complemented her green eyes perfectly.

"Oh, sure," he said.

"I'm sorry about the way Ross talked to you," she went on. "He's not the most modest guy in the world."

"He's a good sailor," said Joey.

"And a better swimmer," Paula said. "He knows it and shows it. He hasn't lost a meet in the three years he's been competing. But you know what I wish?"

He looked into her large eyes. "What?"

"That someone would come along and beat him. His head will never shrink back to its normal size until that happens."

Joey shrugged. "Something I can't understand," he said. "You talk like that about him, yet you go with him."

"Wrong. I don't *go* with him. Riding with him in his sailboat now and then doesn't mean I *go* with him."

"Sorry."

They ate in silence for a minute.

"You know that Gatewood's going to build a new school, don't you?" she said.

"Yes. In a year or so, isn't it?"

All he had heard about it was some talk among the kids in school.

"Right. My parents are going to have a meeting at our house in a couple of weeks. I think your parents are going to be invited. At least I heard their names mentioned."

"Probably," said Joey. "Since we live only a few doors away from you."

"Three," she said, to make it definite. "And a new swimming pool is going to be an issue."

He frowned at her. "A new swimming pool?"

She smiled. "Yes! Wouldn't it be *great* to have a brand new school and a brand new swimming pool? I can hardly wait!"

"I just hope that I can swim better by then," said Joey calmly.

3

JOEY, Yolanda, Mary, and Gabor — all wearing new swimsuits — went in the lake that following Saturday afternoon. The June sun was hot and bright, but it was still too early in the year for it to have warmed the water to a point where swimming was comfortable. It would take another two or three weeks yet before that would happen, providing the weather didn't turn cold again.

None of the four knew how to swim well. Their father had bought Mary and Gabor flotation vests, and of the four children, they were having the most fun. Yolanda was struggling to keep afloat by dog paddling and kicking her feet.

Joey worked at the crawl, the freestyle method of swimming, a little of which he had learned before, and which he preferred over any other. The backstroke, breaststroke, and the other styles of swimming could come later.

Most of Sunday, and then every day after school during the next week, he put on his trunks — a bright red pair with white trim — and went into the water. He found that each time he went in was easier than the time before. He was becoming acclimated to the temperature of the water, and, more important, he was determined that he'd become an expert swimmer as soon as he could.

He had been thinking about why he was so anxious to do so, but wanted to keep the reason to himself for a while. One thing he was able to admit, though, and that was that he owed this new ambition of his to the person he couldn't care less if he ever saw again. Ross Cato. Ross had done nothing *against* him. On the contrary, Ross had done something *for* him; he had given Joey a ride on his sailboat. But Ross had also humiliated him by implying that just because he was shorter than most other boys his age, he would be a born loser when it came to swimming competition.

"You might do all right against those seventh and eighth graders," Ross had said condescendingly. *"Most of them are about your size."*

Well, even though the conversation had taken place weeks ago, those words had been etched into his mind. A lot of nights he had gone to bed thinking about them.

What can I do to make that wise guy eat his words? Joey had asked himself several times since then. He'll have graduated from high school by the time I've really become a good swimmer. But even *good* won't mean that I'd be fast enough to beat him. Ross's long arms and legs are to his advantage. There must be something else that I can learn to do well and beat him at.

Just last night it had come to him what that could be.

"How about tomorrow morning, Joey?" his father asked him at the supper table Friday evening. "You want to wake up at six o'clock and go fishing with me? Maybe we can give each other luck."

His father had gone fishing every evening for an hour or so since Monday, and all he had caught were eight perch, three smallmouth bass, and one lake trout. Two of the perch were too small to bother with, and one of the bass was under legal size, so he had thrown them back into the water, leaving him with a total of nine fish. All were cleaned and put in the freezer, left for more to accumulate to make a fish cookout for the family of six worthwhile.

"Okay," said Joey. "We're not going to be gone all day, are we?"

"Noon at the latest," assured his father.

He had planned on spending most of Saturday in the water. But it was the first time his father had invited him to go fishing with him, and he had thought about trying his luck at it sometime, anyway.

They finished supper, one of Joey's favorite meals — *majorannás tokány* — beef stew with marjoram. For dessert there was still *almásrétes* — apple strudel — left from yesterday. His mother always called the foods she prepared by their Hungarian name, and probably would for the rest of her life.

Half an hour after suppertime, he and his brother and sisters went swimming until sundown. The next morning his father awakened him at six. What a short night, he thought. But, uncomplaining, he dressed, had a breakfast of two scrambled eggs, toast, and milk, and went fishing with his father. They trolled a few miles northward on the east side of the lake, and Joey's father caught two smallmouth bass. Then they crossed the lake and went in the opposite direction for a few miles. This time Joey landed a sixteen-inch northern pike, which, while he was reeling it in, fought hard and bitterly trying to throw the hook that had nabbed it.

"Good boy!" exclaimed his father proudly. "I said you would bring us luck!"

They caught a few small perch, which they threw back, and then returned home. It was close to eleven o'clock, and the sun, almost over their heads now, was getting unbearably hot.

They showed their prize catches to the family — Joey proudly describing the struggle he had pulling in his while they all listened with awe. Then his father cleaned the fish at the dock, tossing the fins, innards, and heads back into the water for scavengers to devour.

"Tonight, my dear Margaret," he said to his wife who stood by watching with the children, "we will have fish."

She smiled. "*Tejfeles sült ponty*," she said, the words rolling with a smooth, musical sound from her lips.

"Yes," he said. "Baked in cream. Ah, yes! I told you Joey would bring us luck, didn't I?"

"Maybe he is a natural fisherman," said his wife.

"Don't count on it," said Joey, amused.

She made them an assortment of sandwiches for lunch. After lunch and what seemed a reasonable lapse of "digesting" time, Joey put on his trunks and went swimming. The water was shallow next to shore. And in checking the depth of it, he found he could walk out almost a hundred feet before it reached his chin. The water was cold, but no matter, as long as he could stand it.

He turned and retraced his steps toward shore until the water was up to his chest, then dove in, and swam the rest of the way. He was still only able to swim about twenty feet before he was tired and out of breath. But after standing for a minute or two, he pushed himself back into the water and continued to swim until he was tired and out of breath again.

He could see that the girls and Gabor had progressed in their swimming, too, although not as much as he. But, then, he was sure that none of them had the determination that he had. None had the purpose to learn to be as good as possible as he. One of these days soon, he would tell them his secret ambition. For a while, though, he would keep it to himself.

They had been in the water only about half an hour when Joey heard one of the girls cry out a name. He looked toward shore and saw Paula Kantella coming down the steps. He felt his heart jump. She was wearing white shorts and a halter. Her hair was loose around her shoulders, being teased by the breeze that was blowing from across the lake.

Another girl was with her. Cindy somebody. Joey had seen her in a couple of his classes but couldn't remember her last name. What he could remember about her was that she talked a lot. She was of slight build, had black hair, wore green shorts, and had skinny legs.

Garfield. That's who she was. Cindy Garfield.

Yolanda and Mary left the water to greet the girls, leaving Gabor behind. He hardly noticed because he was in his glory splashing in the shallow water some ten feet off shore, his flotation vest buckled on him.

Joey went on swimming, taking long overhand strokes while a small part of his mind hoped that Paula would watch him and notice how much he had progressed in the short time since she had last seen him. He still wasn't able to swim far, however, and had to stop, stand up, and catch his breath.

"Joey! Come here a minute!"

He looked toward shore and saw Yolanda motioning to him.

"Be right there!" he called back.

He swam part of the way in, then waded the remaining twenty feet or so. "Hi, Paula. Hi, Cindy," he greeted the girls.

"Hi," they said.

"There's a swim meet at Merton High that starts at two o'clock," Paula went on. "Would you like to see it?"

He thought a moment. "I don't know. What time is it now?"

She looked at her wristwatch. "One forty-five. You still have time. Anyway, even if we're late, there are quite a few races we'd see."

"If you've never seen a swim meet you'll love it," said Cindy, squinting one eye and looking at him through the narrowed lid of the other as the sun beat down on her face. "And if you're not a good swimmer you'll learn a lot, too, just by watching."

So Paula's told you I'm a poor swimmer, he wanted to say to her. Can't be you were looking a minute ago while I was out there, Cindy kid.

"Maybe I would," he said.

"You've improved a lot," Paula said to him. "I saw you out there."

He shrugged.

"Well, I —"

"He's been out there every day this week," Yolanda broke in. "He's crazy, I tell you. You'd think that's all he has to do."

Paula smiled.

"Well, will you come? We can either ride our bikes, hitchhike, or my mother can drive us there."

"I don't have a bike," Joey said.

"I'll have my mother drive us," Paula decided. "Why don't you and Mary come, too, Yolanda?" she invited politely. "I'm sure you'll enjoy it."

"No, thanks, Paula. I'd rather stay here and swim."

"Me, too," said Mary. "And we've got to keep an eye on Gabe."

Paula shrugged. "Okay. See you all later."

Joey hurried to the house to change. He had two reasons for going. One was that he did want to see the meets, and the other, well, he kind of liked being with Paula.

The swimming pool inside Merton High was a glimmering rectangle of blue. Black lines were spaced out at an even parallel on the white bottom to accommodate eight swimmers at a time.

They missed the first event but were in time to see the second, which was already in progress.

"They're in the breaststroke event," observed Cindy as they hurried to find a seat in the already well-packed hall. A couple of kids shouted greetings at them, other kids from Gatewood Central. They waved back and said, "Hi!"

They found three seats halfway up the east side of the pool. Joey sat next to Paula, hoping that Cindy would sit next to her. But Cindy sat beside him, leaving him in between them.

The crowd was a mixture of parents and students, with the students outnumbering the parents by about eight to one. The huge room was a bedlam of chattering voices and yells. It was hard to tell whom anyone was rooting for, unless the student was wearing a shirt with the name of his or her school on it.

The only swimmer Joey thought he would know competing in the breaststroke event was Ross Cato. Even while he looked over the swimmers to identify Ross, Paula's voice broke in beside him. "That's Ross — in the yellow trunks. See where he is, don't you?"

"Yeah," said Joey. "In front."

"By two lengths, at least," added Cindy, sitting on the edge of her seat and clasping white-knuckled hands against her chest. "C'mon, Ross! C'mon, Ross! Isn't he fantastic!"

Joey's attention switched from one swimmer to another, but most of the time it was focused on the leader, Ross. Ross swam with no periods of rest, his elbows pulling down to his sides, hands cupped to pull himself through the water, then extending forward again for the next stroke. Power and strength surged with each forward thrust.

The guy could swim. No doubt about it.

Joey watched closely as Ross, and then the others, made the turn. Both hands touching the wall at the same time, then touching the gutter with both hands. Grab it with one, let go with the other. Pull up close to the wall, tuck knees up, twist, take a breath, throw the arms over, push off, glide, pull through the water with one arm, kick to get back on the surface. Swim again.

Ross won the event, almost two and a half lengths ahead of the second-place finisher. And he probably could've done better if he wanted to, thought Joey.

They watched the butterfly event — which Ross did not compete in— and the backstroke in which he did, and won.

But it was the crawl — the overhand stroke —

that Joey was particularly interested in and that he watched with close scrutiny.

He had not paid much attention to his own swimming style; all he'd been interested in was staying close to the surface of the water and pulling himself forward in it. But now he paid strict attention to the swimmers' actions and movements, particularly to the angle at which their elbows, arms, and legs moved. From the speed that the swimmers were attaining, he realized how vitally important those details were. Bring elbow high out of the water, reach out above the surface of it for the next stroke while taking a short vigorous stroke with the other hand. Repeat the same moves on the other side.

But maybe this style was best for sprints. Long-distance swimming might demand a different style. Joey had to check it out.

Ross won this race too.

4

JOEY thought the *tejfeles sült ponty* was extra-delicious. Along with the fish, his mother had cooked potatoes and *zeller saláta*, celery-root boiled in salted water and served as a salad seasoned with salt, pepper, and mayonnaise. Joey loved that, too. She had also made up a bowl of sliced cucumbers dipped in vinegar and, for dessert, a Hungarian walnut roll she called *diós tekercs*.

When the meal was over, everything was gone except some of the walnut roll, not because it wasn't enjoyed, but because Joey's mother always made more than enough so there would be leftovers for an evening snack or for the next day.

After dinner Joey's father went fishing in his boat, and the kids went swimming. Joey tried to swim the crawl as he had remembered Ross and the other swimmers do it, feeling awkward at first, but gradually believing that he was getting the hang of it. He tried the breaststroke, too, and then the back crawl, neither of which appealed to him as much as the regular freestyle, over-hand swimming stroke.

On Monday he brought home three books from the school library, all devoted to swimming. Along with the books he also took out a brochure about the lakes of New York State. That night, after dark, he read up on Oshawna Lake and made a copy of the map of the lake in pencil on an eight-and-a-half-by-eleven sheet of paper. He indicated the direction it lay by drawing an arrow that pointed north, wrote its length (twenty-one miles), its width at its widest part (two and a quarter miles), and its depth at its deepest part near its center (six hundred and ninety-three feet).

He held the drawing up and looked again at the shape of the lake. About halfway up, about ten miles from the south end, the lake curved slightly to the right. It looked to be the narrowest at that juncture. It was perhaps a mile wide there, or a mile and a half.

Joey didn't have any doubt that at least one person had swum the width of the lake, perhaps even at its widest part. But had anyone ever swum the length of it? The whole twenty-one miles?

Had a kid ever swum it? A kid, say, his age — fourteen.

It would be something if a kid had. Maybe he could find out.

A soft rap on the door interrupted his thoughts.

"Yes?" he said.

"Joey, it's me. You okay?"

"Yes, I'm okay."

It was Yolanda. "May I come in?"

Why not? He couldn't keep his dream a secret forever.

"Sure," he said.

She came in, closed the door softly behind her, and looked at the paper he was holding.

"You've been in here for almost an hour," she said. "Quiet as a mouse."

"I know."

"You drew that? What is it?"

He held it up so she could see it. "Oh. It's Oshawna Lake," she said, recognizing it. "What are those figures for?"

"The length, width — and so on."

"What're you doing it for? Social studies?"

"No. For myself."

"For yourself?" She frowned at him. "I don't get it."

He smiled. "I don't know whether to tell you this or not. You'll think I'm crazy."

"How do you know unless you tell me?"

He lay the drawing on the desk. "Have you wondered why I've been out in the lake so much? Trying to learn to be a good swimmer?"

She shrugged. "Not particularly. Except that I did think you seemed pretty anxious." She went to his bed and sat on it. "Where does the part come in where I might think you're crazy? Oh-oh. I think I can guess."

"One guess."

"You're going to swim across the lake."

"Wrong."

She stared at him. She didn't move. "You're going to swim the length of it." Her voice was barely above a whisper.

He nodded. "Right. At least, I'm going to try. Okay. Think I'm crazy?"

"I don't know. How long is it?"

"Twenty-one miles."

"Twenty-one miles? Oh, wow! Has it ever been done?"

"I don't know. That's what I was thinking about when you knocked on the door. But it wouldn't make any difference. I'm still going to try it, whether anybody has ever done it before or not."

"Joey." Her eyes lighted up.

"Yes?"

"I think you're crazy. But I'm for you — one hundred percent."

He smiled. "Thanks, Yo."

She got off the bed and headed for the door. "Have you told anybody else?" she asked.

"Not yet."

"Then I won't."

"Thanks, again. I keep getting remarks now about my size. I don't need any more about that swim until I'm good and ready."

"Ross Cato say something to you?"

"Nothing much. Called me Peewee and another time Shorty. I really didn't mind that so much except for the way he said them."

"Yeah." She opened the door, looked back at him. "When do you plan on swimming the lake?"

"In another year. Maybe two."

"You'll do it," she said. "You've got what it takes, Joey. You'll do it."

She went out and closed the door gently behind her.

He glanced through the books on competitive swimming, skimming through the pages rapidly to get an idea how the various authors handled the subject. Only one of the three books included chapters on diving, something he didn't want to spend any time on until he mastered long-distance swimming.

He discovered that one of the most important requirements for a competitive swimmer was exercise. Isotonic and isometric were indoor exercises that helped to increase strength, muscle tone, and endurance, he read.

He came across another item he hadn't thought about: the importance of rest periods. Well, that was good. He could certainly use a lot of them.

He needed weights. Barbells, definitely. That meant he needed money, which, in turn, meant that he had to approach his father. *Dad, can I ask you a favor? I need some cash fast. I need to build up my strength so I can accomplish probably the greatest feat I've ever tried. To do that, Dad, I need a set of barbells. That's not bad, is it, for wanting to achieve the next to impossible? Just a set of barbells?*

It all sounded pretty simple as he rehearsed the scene mentally. But he was sure that its reality would be much tougher.

Yes, he'd have to build up his nerve first — get psyched for the moment — and make sure his father was in the right mood. That job as a stone-crusher operator at the quarry was no picnic. He had come home many times from work seething with resentment. The man who was his boss seemed to have little respect for some of the people who worked for him, especially people who lacked at least a high school education, as he seemed to presume Gabor Vass did. Joey had never seen his father's boss, but his father had given him a brief description of the man, enough to paint an indelible picture of him in his mind. Six-foot three, broad and fat bellied, with thick black hair on his arms and chest. Bunko he was called.

"He did it again today," he would come home and say. "Called me a Hungarian runt. Someday I'm going to kill that man."

"You want to go to jail and leave me with all the children?" Joey's mother would say to him in a half-serious tone. "And who would catch all

43

the fish? None of the children likes to fish except you."

It took a comment like that to melt the anger in him.

And when he was in a mood like that, it was best not to talk money to him.

Joey started his indoor exercises the next morning, right after getting out of bed and before breakfast. He lay on his back, raised his legs, and did a running exercise until his thighs began to ache. He rested a while, then did twenty sit-ups, and rested again. He wished he had the barbells.

The next afternoon gray clouds gathered in the sky, and by evening a slow rain began that lasted through the night and the next day. The air had cooled, too, making swimming undesirable.

In the J.C. Penney catalog, he saw barbells listed with a starting price of $13.99. A hydraulic piston muscle exerciser sold for almost twice that amount, and he wished he could have that, too. But for now barbells would do, if he could talk his father into lending him the money.

It was still raining Thursday evening, but Gabor Vass went fishing just the same. "Fish bite better when it rains," he prophesied. "Anybody want to go with me?"

"I'll go!" shouted Gabor, Jr.

"Anybody else?"

"Count me in," said Joey.

"Fine. Make sure there's plenty of room in the freezer, Mama," said her husband cheerfully. "We just might be bringing home a mess of fish."

"When I see it, I will believe it," she said, smiling.

The three of them — father and two sons — put on raincoats and rubbers, gathered up their tackle box and two rods — the only equipment they had so far — and took off in the boat. Joey had an ulterior motive for going. He hadn't had a chance to ask his father yet for money to buy barbells. This might turn out to be the time.

He volunteered to row while his father and Gabor trolled. Gabor got a hit within five minutes.

"I got one!" he yelled. "I got one!"

"Reel it in, Gabor!" cried his father. "Not too fast! Easy . . . easy."

The boy reeled it in and soon had the fish close to the boat, where his father was able to grab it.

"It's a bass," observed his father. "A large-mouth. Good work, Gabor! I knew this was a good time to fish!"

Gabor's face shone with pride as he watched his father remove the hook and lure from the fish's mouth.

Joey smiled. "Must be at least fourteen inches long," he guessed.

"About that, yes," agreed his father, putting the fish on the metal stringer. Then he secured one end of the stringer on a cleat and let the other end of it, to which the fish was attached, dangle freely in the water.

Joey continued to row, feeling the muscles in his arms, legs, and chest tighten each time he pulled on the oars. Right now developing his muscles was more important than catching fish.

At last they reached a spot his father had found to be good fishing on a few occasions. "Stop here, Joey," he said.

"About how deep is it here, Dad?" Joey asked as he lowered the anchor.

"Twelve to fifteen feet," said his father.

They used lures instead of live bait, and Joey's father cast out his line even before the anchor had settled on the bottom. So far the only fish caught was the one by Gabor.

"Can I fish for a while longer?" he asked his father hopefully.

"Can you cast without getting a hook caught in somebody's head?" his father said.

"Sure, I can."

His father grinned. "Okay. For a while."

"Dad, can I ask you something?" Joey said.

His father looked at him. "You think I should buy Gabor a rod and reel. I know."

"No, it isn't that. It's . . . well, I need some money."

"Oh? How much and for what?"

"About fourteen dollars. For barbells. I'll try to find a job and pay you back."

"That's nice of you. Two questions: Why do you want barbells, and what kind of job do you think you can find?"

"I want to work out," said Joey. "And I'm sure I can find a job. Cutting people's lawns, washing windows. I know kids from school who do jobs like that all the time."

"Okay, fine. But what is this about exercise? You want to be Mr. America?"

Joey smiled. "No."

"Then what?"

Joey hesitated.

"Wait a minute, I got something," said his father, and reeled in a fifteen-inch speckled trout. "Ain't that a beauty!" he cried happily. "There you go, Gabor! The old man caught one, too!"

Gabor laughed.

Joey's father strung up the trout. "There," he said, putting the stringer back into the water. "The bass needed company. Now," he addressed Joey as he cast the line out over the water again, "back to — what were we talking about?"

"Barbells," said Joey.

"Oh, yes. You were going to tell me why you wanted to work out."

Joey looked thoughtfully out over the lake. It stretched out for miles like a slightly rippled mirror. "I'm planning on swimming this lake, Dad," he said. "From one end of it to the other."

His father stared at him. Just for a moment, the hand that was reeling in the line slowly had stopped. Presently it started turning again.

"You know how long this lake is?"

"Twenty-one miles," replied Joey.

"Twenty-one miles," his father echoed. "And you think you can swim it."

"I want to try it."

"Why?" asked his father. "Why would you want to do that, my boy?"

"To prove that I can do it," said Joey.

His father nodded. "To prove that you can do

it," he echoed thoughtfully. "To prove it to whom? Yourself?"

"Myself. And maybe others, too."

"You must have learned to swim pretty good already."

"Oh, I've got a lot to learn yet. But what I've got to do now is develop my body. I need to exercise every day, and barbells will be a big help."

"How do you know?"

"I read it in books I got from the library."

"Oh. So you have studied up on it?"

"Right."

"Well, that much is good."

"It'll be another year — maybe two — before I'll be ready to swim it," Joey explained. "Twenty-one miles is a long way."

Something warm lay deep in his father's eyes. "It sure is," he agreed. "Okay. Get the barbells. You might as well start working on that body of yours right away. I'm small, too. Too damn small. I've got muscles, but most of them are in my head. My brains are muscle-bound, Joey. That's why I'm a stone crusher. You don't need brains to be a stone crusher."

"Come on, Dad. I don't think —"

"Oh-oh, I think I've got a fish, Daddy!" Gabor cried enthusiastically.

His rod was bending like a rainbow, the line tautening.

"You sure have, Gabor," observed his father. "Reel it in. Easy, now. Easy. Don't lose him."

It was another speckled trout. A fourteen incher.

5

JOEY BOUGHT a set of barbells the next day after school from the J.C. Penney store in town. He used his mother's credit card to buy it, promising he'd pay her back as soon as he got a job. His father and mother had decided this was simpler than giving him cash, which they seldom had in the house anyway. Joey and his father had told her last night after they had returned from fishing what he intended to do. But her sentiments had been different from his father's.

"What? Swim that lake?" she had said, her voice almost an octave higher than normal as she stared at him. "You are just a boy! It is too much for a man even! You will drown before you get five miles!"

"I'll have someone go alongside me with a boat," explained Joey. "If I get real tired, or get sick, I'll stop. Don't worry, Mom. I'm not that dumb."

"You are dumb if you think you're going to swim that lake," she told him.

But she let him have the credit card, and he bought the barbells. That night he started using them, following the instructions in the books to make sure he was doing everything right. Lifting the barbells straight over his head, extending them horizontally, bending over and touching them to the floor, then repeating the routine over and over again until his body, naked except for the swim trunks, was aching and drenched with sweat.

He showered afterwards, put on clean underwear, and felt like a million. But the next day every joint and muscle in his body screamed with pain. He knew it would take several days of exercising before he'd feel normal again.

The meeting regarding the new school took place at Paula Kantella's house at seven-thirty on June 29, a week after graduation day. Joey hadn't intended to go to it. It was expected that including a swimming pool in the overall plan was a big factor in whether the plan was going to be accepted. The pool was going to cost about four hundred thousand dollars, a lot of money in the opinion of many of the city's taxpayers who were already paying "through the nose," as many of them put it. Although Joey liked to see a swimming pool included in the plans for the new school, he couldn't see himself giving his opinion to the adults who were going to be there. But Paula had asked him to come anyway, and it didn't take much persuasion from her to accept her invitation.

Twenty people attended, partially filling up the large living room and dining room. The two rooms connected and were almost like one huge room. Mrs. Townsend, a school representative who was a member of the board of education, started off by presenting the facts and figures and showing a layout of the proposed school. Joey and Paula sat on chairs in the background, listening intently to her clear, concise remarks. She spoke plainly and well, obviously knowing her topic inside and out.

A question of the courtyard came up, which she settled quite easily with a few pleasant, straightforward answers. Someone also mentioned the laboratory for the science class. How much would the equipment cost for it? Would there be enough ventilation for it, because, as this parent explained, "my son's complained about the ventilation of the one he's been in for two years. There's been complaints on top of complaints, promises on top of promises to get it taken care of, yet nothing's been done."

"The science lab will be one of the most up-to-date in the country," promised Mrs. Townsend. "It'll have enough chairs and tables to accommodate thirty students. Equipment will be sophisticated but not terribly expensive. And the room will be adequately ventilated. You can bet on it."

Then the inevitable question came up. "Can't the swimming pool be put in for a lot less than four hundred thousand dollars? Man, that's a lot of money just to let a few kids swim."

"Have you conducted any surveys, Mr. Williams?" Mrs. Townsend asked. "Have you checked the costs of the installation of a swimming pool in schools around the state? They are expensive, and four hundred thousand dollars is quite a good deal less than some of them cost."

"I can't believe it," another voice cut in. "You know how much four hundred thousand dollars is? That's almost a half a million hard, solid bucks!"

"I know how much four hundred thousand dollars is, sir," said Mrs. Townsend, without raising her voice. "Nowadays it doesn't go very far when you're thinking big — and building a brand new high school is thinking big."

"My children swim in the lake, Mrs. Townsend," a familiar, accented voice chimed in. "I know that the lake water is cold most of the year round, but it does not cost them anything to swim in it. And my taxes are already plenty high just because our home is by the lake. There are also beaches on the lake where children and their parents can go to swim, and that does not cost them anything. I think that a swimming pool in the school is nice, yes. But most of the people in Gatewood have to work hard for their money. My wife and I have four children. I don't make so much money as maybe some other man in this room makes. The extra tax that a big, nice swimming pool would cost us every year would be another bite into our pocketbooks just so a few children could swim all year round."

Joey felt himself staring at his father proudly, listening to the words spilling slowly from his father's lips — words that truly came from his heart and caught the attention of everyone in the room. The strong Hungarian accent was highly noticeable; Joey was sure that very few of the people there knew his father and mother and were not aware until now that they — his father, anyway — couldn't speak English very well. But they certainly should have been able to understand what he had meant.

"I understand your feelings, sir," said Mrs. Townsend. "And I truly appreciate your views. But I'd like to remind you — and others here — that during competitive swimming meets, there will be an admission charge. Money will be used to pay for the electricity to light the big room and keep the water heated —"

"But what has that got to do with the taxes, Mrs. Townsend?" spoke up another voice.

"They'll still be reaching into our pockets for more money, Mrs. Townsend."

A warm hand touched Joey's arm.

"Joey, let's go out on the porch," Paula whispered into his ear.

Quietly they got up and tiptoed out of the room. The door leading to the wide, screened-in porch was open. They stepped through it, found chairs next to each other, and slumped into them.

"Sounds like it's going to be a long, dragged-out meeting," said Joey.

Paula smiled. "Could be. Your dad is really against the swimming pool, isn't he?"

"So's my mother," admitted Joey. "I knew that all along."

"How do you feel about it?"

"Oh, heck, I'd like to have one, sure. But I'm not a family man. I'm just a fourteen-year-old kid who doesn't have to support a family and pay taxes. Maybe if I were in my parents' shoes, I'd see it their way, too."

"Yes, I suppose you're right. I gather your father doesn't earn much money. What does he do?"

Joey wished she hadn't asked that. This was one of the small things that bothered him to talk about — his parents' heritage and what his father did to earn an income.

"He's a stone crusher," he said.

"A stone crusher? Where?"

"At the Gatewood Crushed Stone Company. He operates a machine that crushes the big stones after they're brought by trucks to his place and dumped. The stones are crushed down to different sizes and sold by the ton."

"Oh. That's what he does," she said.

"Yes. That's what he does."

"I guess you know what my father does," she said.

"He's an engineer, isn't he?"

"Yes. For an air-conditioning plant. I think he makes a lot of money."

"Probably twice as much as my father does."

"I don't know exactly," said Paula. "But when we bought a new TV set just before Christmas, Dad paid cash for it."

"Wow," said Joey. "I guess if you've got it, fine."

"You know, it's funny," she said. "Till just this minute, I never gave money much thought. I thought it was something people had enough of without worrying about how much anything costs. Guess I'm pretty dumb. Your father gave a nice speech in there, Joey. I'd be proud of him if I were you."

"Thanks, Paula. I am."

They were quiet for a while, and he suddenly remembered that he had never told her about his ambition to swim the length of Oshawna Lake. He had wanted it to be a secret in the beginning, but since he had improved so much he didn't think it was necessary any longer.

He broke the news to her gently. She looked at him, surprised at first, but only for a minute.

"Hey, that's great, Joey!" she exclaimed. "I mean — wow! That's really great! When did you decide to do that?"

He smiled.

"This summer. I had to be sure. I didn't want anyone to know at first."

"Oh, Joey!" Her face beamed. "I think that

would really be an accomplishment! I really do!"

Later they were called in for doughnuts, and they knew that the evening discussion about the new school was over.

While people ate the refreshments, they continued to talk and ask questions. What did most of the town think about having a swimming pool included in the plan? Was Mrs. Townsend going to be able to sway votes to her side, or was the cost going to be too high for most people to accept?

Joey and everybody else interested in the answers wouldn't know until the voting on the issue was done and counted.

Joey got a summer job mowing the lawn and washing windows for Mrs. Kenny, a widow who lived only a few doors away. He worked hard on his exercises, spending half an hour in the morning at them and half an hour in the afternoon. Looking at his reflection in the mirror, he couldn't really tell if his muscles were developing. But he was sure they were. You couldn't spend an hour a day doing solid exercises, using barbells most of the time, without changes taking place in your body.

He swam every day, extending the distance

from about fifty yards to seventy-five, from seventy-five to a hundred, from a hundred to two hundred. He swam parallel to the shoreline, keeping within a hundred feet of shore so that if anything happened — if he got a cramp in his legs or in his stomach — he'd be close enough to swim to shallow water and stand up. Of course he would try to work the cramp out of his legs or feet first before coming in to shore. But if he couldn't, shallow water would be just a few yards away.

A few days later, he turned down an invitation to go sailing with Ross and Paula. It was Ross who asked him; the invitation came while the two were rowing out to the sailboat and saw him swimming. But he had a hunch it was Paula's idea. There was something about the smile she gave him, something about that wave.

But he wasn't keen about Ross's company. He didn't like some of the things Ross said or the way he said them. Those cracks about Joey's height, for example.

There was something else he didn't like about Ross. It wasn't until recently that he began to realize it. He didn't like the way Ross looked at Paula.

I guess I'm jealous, he admitted to himself.

The people voted for the new school on July 6. Included was a referendum about the swimming pool.

The next day, on Friday, an article published in the *Gatewood Courier* reported that the school bond issue had been passed, but the referendum to include a swimming pool had been turned down by a vote of three to one.

THE SECOND YEAR

1

THE WINTER was the most severe one that had struck the county in twenty years. Joey thought it would never end.

One morning the Vass family found a snow-drift fifteen feet high piled up in front of their back door, and it had taken the whole family almost all day to tunnel a hole through it to get to the driveway. The temperature hovered below zero most of January and February, and when the weather began to warm up, there were threats of flooding. The Chemung River rose until it overran its banks. Water entered the cellars of many of the homes, but the level didn't rise high enough to cause any serious damage. It was nothing like the havoc that tropical storm Agnes had caused back in the early 1970s when the rampaging river had demolished homes, properties, and farms.

Because of the uniqueness of the Oshawna Lake watershed — hundreds of streams around the long body of water funneled melted snow down into it — the lake level rose three feet above normal. It caused damage to cottages built close to the water's edge and to docks and boat houses.

What bothered Joey was all the garbage that had been washed down into the water, the raw sewage, the foam along the lake's edge, the bad smell, the sludge, the thousands of dead fish. This was April. Could all that stuff be cleaned up by June so that he could start swimming again?

He had exercised all winter, missing only three days, when he had caught a severe cold and had to take time off from school. He had even gone so far as to have his father help him make a bench on which he could lie on his stomach and practice coordinating his arm and leg action.

But it was the use of the barbells that had built up his muscle tone. Curling — lifting the barbells up from his thighs to his shoulders while keeping his elbows down — strengthened his forearms and biceps. He would do this six times, rest for a minute, and do it again.

On the bench he did the back press. Lying on it on his back, with his feet on the floor, he would lift the barbells from the level of his chest straight up to arm's length, bring them down, lift them up again. This, too, he would do six times, rest, and six times again.

Holding the barbells across the back of his neck, keeping his back straight and bending his knees, he also did half-knee bends, which strengthened his legs, developed his chest, and increased his lung capacity.

To build up his calf muscles, he stood with his feet slightly apart, held the barbells across the back of his neck, and kept his body up arrow-straight. Then slowly he would raise his heels until he was standing only on his toes. Up, down; up, down. Six times, rest; six times, rest again.

Every day. *Every day*.

He had gained seven pounds. He now tipped the scales, in the raw, at one hundred and twenty-eight pounds.

By the middle of May, the lake had receded almost to its normal level. Much of the muddiness cleared up, garbage had sunk to the bottom, driftwood had washed ashore. It was still too cold to swim in.

The fear came over Joey that the summer wouldn't be long enough for him to get in the amount of swimming he needed. *He still had not yet swum even a mile at one time. And the lake was twenty-one miles long.*

Twenty-one miles!

Joey read some statistics about long-distance swimming. Back in August 1872, a J. B. Johnson had tried — but failed — to swim the English Channel. The distance — from Dover, England, to Calais, France — was twenty-two miles. It was the narrowest part of the channel.

In August 1875, a Captain Matthew Webb swam it successfully, completing an approximate fifty-mile zigzag course, through strong current and rough seas, in twenty-one hours and forty-five minutes. The swim was done in August because weather conditions were most favorable during that month.

In 1926 Gertrude Ederle became the first woman to swim the channel, cutting Captain Webb's time by almost two hours. She had swum the crawl style, while Webb had swum the breaststroke, the most popular stroke of his time.

But the longest swim on record was two hundred and eighty-eight miles. Clarence Giles had swum the Yellowstone River from Glendive, Montana, to Billings in seventy-one hours and three minutes, June 30 to July 3, 1939.

Two hundred and eighty-eight miles! thought Joey. The English Channel is twenty-two miles wide. And I'm thinking of swimming twenty-one miles.

I really might be able to do it.

It was on the third Wednesday of May when Joey's father sprang a surprise on his family. Joey noticed how quiet his father was during supper, quieter than usual, and assumed that something had happened at work again that annoyed him. Things weren't any better at the stone-crushing company than they were before. Sometimes Joey thought they were worse.

But it wasn't the job that was on his father's mind.

"There is a boat for sale I want to look at," his father said, drawing the attention of everyone to him. "I saw the advertisement in this morning's paper. If I like it, I am going to buy it."

"So that is why you have been quiet?" said his wife. "You was thinking about the boat?"

"Yes. The one I have is too small. I would like a bigger one with a motor."

"How much is it?"

"Two hundred and seventy-five dollars. That does not sound bad, but maybe I could talk the man into selling it to me for even less — maybe two fifty."

Joey laughed. "I bet you can, Dad."

"It's the Magyar in him," said Joey's mother, smiling.

"It's his charm, Mom," interposed Yolanda. "Wasn't it his charm that got you to marry him?"

"His charm? Yes, I suppose it was. But I have not seen much of it lately."

"It's because of his job, Mom," Mary added. "You know how it's been bothering him."

Joey's father chuckled. "What do you know about my job, my little *egér?*"

She shrugged. "Not much," she admitted. "But enough."

"I am going to call up the man and see if he'll be home," said Joey's father. "You want to come with me, Joey?"

"Yes, I'll go with you, Dad."

"Can't I go, too, Daddy?" Gabor pleaded.

"Why not? The more the merrier."

"Take the girls, too," said Joey's mother. "Then the man will see how big a family you have and will sell you the boat for half the price he is asking."

"Now that is going too far, Margaret," said her husband, pretending irritation. "But it is a good idea," he added, smiling.

"Maybe the man needs the money, too," said Joey's mother. "Maybe that is why he wants to sell his boat."

"We'll see," replied her husband. "Well, I will make the call."

He made it, and a few seconds later hung up, smiling jovially. "All who are going with me, get ready!"

The children, all but Yolanda, scrambled off to get their coats. Before flying out of earshot, Joey heard his father say to his mother, "You sure you don't want to come, *édes?*"

"I am sure," she said. "I have a hundred things to do, starting with the dishes. Yolanda, you're not going?"

"No, Mom. You go with them," insisted Yolanda. "I'll stay here and do the dishes. Go on. You don't get out enough, anyway."

"She's right, Margaret," said Joey's father. "Come on. The fresh air will do you good."

Joey paused a little longer, waiting to hear what his mother was going to say.

"Get my sweater, Yolanda," she finally decided. "I'll brush my hair. It looks like a mop."

Joey ran to get his, a smile splitting his face from ear to ear.

In ten minutes they were on their way, their destination an address in the country some fifteen miles beyond Gatewood. They found it without difficulty, and saw the object of their trip sitting on a trailer in the back yard, a hand-printed For Sale sign taped on its bow. It was a white, fiberglass boat with a small Johnson engine. The extra four feet in length over their rowboat, and the addition of the engine, would make the purchase a definite advancement.

A tall, gangling man came from the house, wearing gray overalls and a battered straw hat. "Hi, ya," he greeted. "You the gent who called about the boat?"

"I am," said Joey's father.

"Well, there's the boat," said the man. "It's all set to go. It's five years old, but it runs like a top. You'll be very satisfied with it, I guarantee."

"May I ask you a question, please?" asked Joey's father.

"Why, sure." The man's sun-browned, leathery face broke into a smile.

"Why do you want to sell a nice boat like that?"

"Why? Because the doctor told me I'd better quit fishing and hunting if I want to keep enjoying a longer life, that's why. I had a stroke, you see. I'm lucky to be alive."

"Oh, I'm sorry."

"So am I. But that's the way the ball bounces."

Joey's father didn't dicker over the price of the boat. The man filled out the registration papers, signed a bill of sale, and took the check.

"You don't have a hitch, do you?" he observed. "Well, I can take the boat to your place right now — follow you there, if you want me to — or do it first thing in the morning."

"Right now will be fine, if you have the time," said Joey's father.

"I have plenty of time. Give me a few minutes."

"Sure," said Joey's father.

As the man tramped up the path toward the tall, two-and-a-half-story house. Joey's father turned and faced his wife and children.

"I feel guilty," he said.

"Why?" said his wife. "You paid him what he asked for, didn't you?"

"Yes. But I came out here wanting to demand he lower his price. I didn't know he was sick, or else —"

"But you didn't do it, *édes*. You had respect for him. I — I admire you for that."

He smiled. "It is a fair price, I'm sure."

Joey clutched his hand, squeezed it affectionately. "You're okay, Dad," he said, feeling his throat tightening up. "You're really okay."

His father, still smiling, returned the squeeze.

2

A WIND made the lake choppy the following evening, but Joey's father was intent on going fishing anyway. There were a couple of bays on the east shore where the water was well protected. As long as the wind was blowing from the east, the water there would be virtually smooth. They took their raincoats, however, just in case.

His father's guess was right about the conditions, as he and Joey discovered when they arrived there. It was about ten past six. The air was warm, the sky a mass of slow-moving gray clouds that seemed to be working up into a giant lather.

"It looks as if we're going to have a storm,

Dad," observed Joey, casting out his line. It whirred loudly as it spun off the reel.

"It's hard to tell," said his father. "Maybe it will blow away and not touch us."

Fifteen minutes later, Joey felt a tug on his line, yanked the rod, knew he had something, and started to reel it in.

"Got one, Dad!" he said.

"Good boy."

He soon hauled in a jackperch. Not long after that, drops of rain began to fall as dark clouds began to swirl over their heads. The wind had picked up perceptibly, too.

"We better head for home," said Joey's father. "Reel in your line, Joey."

They both reeled in their lines, lay the rods down on the floor, and put on their raincoats. Then Joey lifted up the only fish they had caught and placed it beside the rods.

His father started the engine, and they headed for home. By the time they had the boat safely upon on shore and the engine and prop up, the rain was coming down in torrents.

"You've gotten pretty strong over the winter months," said Joey's father, ignoring the rain that battered his hat and shoulders. "I saw how you pulled up the boat."

"I exercise every day, Dad," said Joey.

"You still think you want to swim the lake?"

" 'Course, I do."

His father shook his head. "Sometimes I think it is all right, but sometimes I think it isn't."

"Why? I'm going to have a boat go alongside me. Ours. Yolanda can drive it. That okay with you, Dad?"

"Sure, but I don't know, Joey. It could be dangerous, that long swim."

"I tell you, Dad, there's nothing to worry about. I've looked into it very thoroughly. And as soon as the water warms up, I'm going to start swimming again."

Joey got the fish. "Shall I clean it before I take it up to the house?"

"Better. What the hell, you can't get any wetter. And it's better to put the fish into the freezer cleaned than not cleaned."

"Right."

The expression on his father's face changed. Something different entered the mild, friendly eyes. "I bet you wished that the people had voted for a swimming pool in the new school, didn't you?" he said.

"Sometimes I have," Joey admitted.

"But you understand why I was against it, don't you? Why most of the people voted against it?"

"Oh, sure. Because it cost too much."

"Yes. That would have meant a higher tax. Four hundred thousand dollars is an awful lot of money for a swimming pool."

"I know, Dad."

"Well, I thought you did. Okay, clean your fish."

He turned and went on to the steps while Joey got the knife out of the tackle box, stepped up onto the dock, and proceeded to clean the fish. His father had surprised him by bringing up the subject of the swimming pool. Joey guessed that his father knew that if there had been a swimming pool built in the almost completed new school, Joey would have been able to swim there nearly every day instead of in the lake where he could swim only when the water was warm enough. A daily swim would be the perfect solution in training for the long twenty-one-mile swim.

He's thinking of me, thought Joey. That's the important thing.

Joey was in his room the following afternoon, doing his exercises with the barbells, when a knock sounded on the door.

"Joey, it's me," said a familiar voice. "Are you decent?"

"I'm decent, Aunt Liza," he said, recognizing her voice. He made a sour face, but then tried to look pleasant as she entered the room.

Under most circumstances he didn't mind his aunt's coming to the house for a visit; his mother and father were the only people she knew with whom she could speak Hungarian. But he was sure that her wanting to see him while he was exercising meant something uncomfortable was about to come up.

He was doing sit-ups when she entered.

"Hello, Joey," she greeted him.

"Hello, Aunt Liza."

He kept exercising as if she weren't there.

"Joey, can I talk to you a minute?"

He stopped. "Sure. You want to sit down?"

"Thank you." She sat down on his chair.

"Didn't you work today?" he asked.

"Yes. But I quit early. I had a dentist appointment."

"You've been there already?"

"Yes. Joey, should I talk to you in English instead of Hungarian?"

"I don't care. But I can understand English better. What are you going to talk to me about? That swim I'm going to do?"

"Yes."

"Oh, Aunt Liza," he said impatiently. "I'm going to do it, no matter what you say. I've *got* to do it, don't you understand? I've got to swim that lake, Aunt Liza."

"If you do, you will make me very unhappy, Joey. I will worry for you every minute. And your mother will worry for you. And your father, too."

"They both know I'm going through with it, Aunt Liza," he said. "And they aren't worried, not anywhere as much as you seem to think. I'm not going to swim the Atlantic Ocean, Aunt Liza. It's just going to be Oshawna Lake, and I'm going to have a boat alongside of me every minute of the time. There's nothing to be worried about. Nothing."

"You don't know how my Janos died, do you?"

"I know he drowned," said Joey.

"Yes, he drowned. And he was a good swimmer, did you know that? He was a very *fine* swimmer, Janos was."

"Dad told me," said Joey.

"He drowned in four feet of water," said his aunt. "Did he tell you that, too?"

"I don't think so."

"When — when he was pulled out of the

water —" Her voice broke, and she reached into her purse for a handkerchief and touched it to the tears that came to her eyes.

"Aunt Liza, you don't have to tell me anymore about Janos," said Joey. "I know how you feel about him."

"I — I don't want you to risk your life, too," she stammered, and blew her nose. "You want your mother and father to go through the pains and heartaches I and your uncle went through? They will never get over it. Never."

"If I don't swim that lake, Aunt Liza, then I'll feel that —" He paused, not knowing how to continue. Why say more to her? No matter what he said, she would still insist he was crazy to attempt swimming Oshawna Lake.

"I can't understand why," she went on, looking at him as if suddenly she had seen a new and different side of him. "Why do you think you have to swim that lake? My God! Yolanda said it is twenty-one miles long. Twenty-one miles! Did you know that there were many swimmers who tried to swim across the English Channel and could not? And the English Channel is almost the same distance."

"But you can't compare the English Channel with Oshawna Lake," Joey said.

"Why not?"

"The English Channel is controlled by tides and winds. It moves a lot faster than Oshawna Lake because it flows into the North Sea. And it's a lot colder. It hardly gets above sixty degrees even during the hottest months of the year. Oshawna gets up into the seventies, and sometimes eighties. It's been recorded at eighty-one. It has an outlet, too, but the water flows so slowly you'd hardly notice it. You just can't compare the two, Aunt Liza."

She stared at him. "You have read a lot about it, haven't you?"

"Yes, I have."

"What's the difference? Why is it so important to you? You want to break a world record or something, is that it? You want to risk your life to get your name in that book — what is the name of it? Guinness?"

"I guess so."

"Well? Is that it? You want your name in that book?"

"No, Aunt Liza. I don't want my name in that book. But, you're right, in a way. I want to prove something."

"Oh. Now it is beginning to come out. Okay, so what is it you want to prove?"

"That I can do something a lot of other people can't," he confessed. "That just because I'm small doesn't mean I'm a nothing."

"And who says you're a nothing?"

"Nobody. But there are people who call me Peewee, and Shorty, and Shortjob, and Squirt, and make remarks about my height. It bothers me, and I want to do something about it."

She looked at him as if she were trying to see into his mind. Slowly she shook her head. "Joey no matter what you will do, there will always be people who will call you such names. A tall, skinny man they will call Slim. Sometimes they will call him Fatso. A man with a big belly they will call Fatso. Sometimes they will call him Slim. You know what they call your Uncle Janos at his job? Hunky. Because he is Hungarian. Some people just do not care about calling other people by their real names. It is much easier to say Slim, or Fatso, or Hunky. You know what I mean?"

He nodded. "Yes, Aunt Liza," he said. "But after I swim that lake, it just won't be the same."

"You're wrong, Joey."

"Okay. I'm wrong. But I'm still going to swim it."

She got off the chair. "I hope you change your mind before that day comes."

He smiled. "I doubt that I will, Aunt Liza."

She smiled back. "You're a little devil," she said.

"See?" he said. "You called me little."

"I know." She grinned impishly at him and left the room.

3

FOR SEVERAL DAYS during the middle of May, the sun beat down like a flaming torch. It warmed up the surface of the lake enough for Joey and his brother and sisters to go out for their first swim of the year. Joey, an adept free-style swimmer by now, swam out almost a hundred yards; then he found that the water had cooled several degrees. But the feel of it, and the realization that each day from now on meant better and warmer weather, thrilled him. He frolicked about like a young colt let out to pasture after having been cooped up in a stall all winter. He laughed and yelled, and waved to Yolanda to swim out to him. She started to, came out about halfway, then turned and swam back.

Oh, wow! He thought. For a while there I really thought she was going to!

He was glad she didn't. It might've been too far for her. He was at least a hundred yards out now, treading water, and feeling the real coldness of it on his thighs and legs. He felt great.

He started to swim back in toward shore when the sound of a powerboat reached his ears. He looked around and saw the boat approaching toward him, waves spouting from either side of its bow like white wings. He caught a glimpse of a water skier behind it.

He hadn't swum more than fifty feet when the boat started to sweep behind him, and a voice shouted, "Joeeeey!"

He stopped swimming and looked back. A grin came over his face as he recognized Ross Cato behind the wheel of the boat, Paula at the stern, and Cindy on the skis.

"Hi!" he yelled, waving back.

Cindy removed a hand from the short stick she was hanging onto and waved to him.

Joey tried not to let Paula's being with Ross bother him. After all, Cindy was with them, too. It didn't mean anything.

He continued to swim back to shore, but before he got there, he saw that Ross had swung the boat around in a wide circle and was coming in to shore ahead of him. Ross cut the engine, and Cindy, sweeping in on her skis behind the boat, slowed down quickly and sank to her thighs in the water.

After an exchange of greetings, Paula asked Joey if he'd care to try water skiing.

"Sure," he said willingly.

"Okay. Put on that preserver," said Paula.

He put it on, then secured his feet to the skis, listened to Cindy's and Paula's chorus of suggestions, and took off behind Ross's expert piloting of the boat. He didn't make it up on the skis on the first two tries, but on the third try he was up on them and stayed up for over two minutes before Ross's slow turn, which forced him to ride the waves that the boat subsequently created, made him lose his balance and fall.

He managed to get on the skis again and rode for a few more minutes before Ross headed back for shore. This time Yolanda tried her skill at it, succeeding after a few attempts, and finally Mary tried it.

Joey, standing next to Cindy and Yolanda, watched as his younger sister got up, fell, got up again, and fell again.

"She won't make it," said Joey.

"She will, too," said Yolanda.

She did make it. But for only a few seconds. She went down, both skis going into an X under her. Ross quickly cut down the power and swung the boat around.

"I think she's hurt," Yolanda said anxiously.

"Oh, no!" Cindy moaned.

Joey watched, his heart pounding. His first thought was what his mother would say. "It's the last time," that's what she'd say. "The last time you get on water skis."

And Aunt Liza? "I told you!" she'd cry. "That lake is dangerous! She was lucky she didn't get killed!"

"They're both lifting her into the boat," Yolanda said breathlessly. "Oh, dear, I hope she's not hurt bad."

"Maybe she's not hurt at all," said Joey. "Maybe she's just tired."

That's what he hoped, but he suspected the worse. Both Ross and Paula were tending to her, as if trying to make her comfortable. Then Ross got back behind the wheel and maneuvered the craft so that Paula could pick the skis out of the water. In a moment they were speeding in toward shore.

"Oh, man," said Joey nervously. "Why did we let her try it? She's too young."

"She isn't too young," countered Yolanda. "I've seen lots of kids her age water skiing. It's just her luck."

"And ours," added Joey.

He and Yolanda ran up on the dock, waited for the boat to come up alongside it, and grabbed it. Ross shut the engine off and secured the boat to cleats fore and aft.

Joey saw blood oozing from a small cut on the side of Mary's head as she stepped out of the boat.

"Your head's bleeding," said Joey, worriedly, helping her out.

"Never mind. I'm okay."

"Are you hurt anywhere else?" asked Yolanda.

"No!" she snapped. "I told you I'm okay!"

"Just the same you'd better get up to the house and have that taken care of," Joey advised.

"I'm sorry about this," cried Paula, her face pale as paper. "Oh, I'm so sorry about this."

"It's not your fault," said Ross. "Quit moaning, will you?"

"But I was the one who asked her if she wanted to ski."

"And she said yes. So what? It could happen to anybody."

"Don't worry about it, Paula," said Joey. "She'll be all right."

Yolanda removed the life preserver from Mary, then took her sister's hand, and started to lead her hurriedly off the dock and toward the steps.

"I'm going with her," said Paula.

"You don't have to," Joey told her. "It's just a cut. A bandage will take care of it."

"But your mother will blame me," exclaimed Paula, stepping out of the boat. "I know she will."

"No, she won't."

"Let her go," declared Ross, irritably. "You're not going to change her mind."

Joey watched her run off the dock and catch up to the girls.

"I guess you're right," he said.

He looked back at Ross. Their eyes met, and a wide grin came over the tall boy's tanned face.

"Hey, man, Paula tells me you're going to swim Oshawna Lake. The whole twenty-one miles of it. That right?"

Joey nodded. "I'm going to try," he said.

"That takes a lot of guts, man."

"Maybe."

"Maybe, hell. I know it does. I wouldn't try it."

"You might do it."

"Not me. I'm a sprinter."

Joey shrugged.

Ross's eyes searched his curiously. "Why in hell do you want to swim the length of it for, anyway? Just for the fun of it, or is somebody going to pay you a chunk?"

"Maybe the first part of that is the answer," replied Joey.

"You're going to swim it just for the fun of it?" Ross stared at him long and hard.

"Yes."

"You must be nuts. You won't make it. You'll *never* make it. Hell, man, you just learned to swim last year, didn't you?"

"I'll make it," said Joey calmly.

Ross frowned. "We'll see," he said.

Paula and Cindy returned from the house a few minutes later. Cindy seemed cheerful — but she always seemed to be that way, no matter what happened — so Joey couldn't tell from her expression what had gone on up at the house.

But Paula showed concern. Her eyes were red, as if she'd been crying.

"How is she?" Ross asked.

"Okay," Cindy answered. "Mrs. Vass washed the cut, put some stuff on it, and covered it with a bandage. She'll be okay."

Paula said nothing. She went past Joey to the boat, stepped into it, and sat down on one of the cushioned seats. She rested an elbow on the side, placed a curved forefinger against her mouth, and stared into space.

"I know she will. I just feel it's my fault she's hurt, that's all."

Ross grinned. "It's that motherly instinct," he said to Joey. "You know what I mean?"

He kicked over the engine. It sprang to life. "See you!" he yelled. Putting the boat in reverse, he backed it around the dock and then shoved the throttle forward. The engine roared as the craft shot ahead. Joey waved to them, then turned and headed for the steps.

The remainder of the spring passed quickly, and in June Joey took final exams and suffered through two days of anguish as he waited for a report on his mark in Chemistry I. He had passed the other subjects with better than average marks, but Chemistry I was the killer. He'd be hurt, but not surprised, if he got a failing mark in it.

He didn't. On the evening of the second day

after the exam, he called Mrs. Berkoltz, his teacher. She told him that he had scored a seventy-six. His anguish over, he didn't hesitate to ask her how Paula had done, since both of them were in the same class.

"I don't give out other students' marks. Why don't you call her yourself?" Mrs. Berkoltz suggested.

"Did she call you?" he asked.

"Yes."

"Okay. Thanks, Mrs. Berkoltz."

"You're welcome, Joseph."

He hung up, realizing how excited he must have sounded to her. What's the matter with me? he thought. I think of Paula, and I get all funny inside. Heck, she doesn't care for me. She's Ross's girl.

He waited until he calmed down a little and then dialed the number he had memorized quite some time ago. Again he felt a stirring in his body as he heard her phone ringing. Then the ringing stopped, and a familiar voice said, "Hello?"

"Paula?"

"Yes! Joey?"

"Right. How'd you make out in Chem?"

"I passed! I had eighty-one! Did you call Mrs. Berkoltz?"

"Yeah. Just a little while ago. I got a seventy-six. And I feel lucky. I was afraid I had flunked it."

She chuckled. "You? Phooey! She wouldn't flunk you, Joey!"

"Ha! Oh, no? That's what you think."

"I don't know about you," said Paula. "You have so little faith in yourself. Well, except for that long swim you're planning on. When will the spectacular event be, anyway? This year?"

"No. Next year."

"It's going to be a long winter."

"I know. Well, see you."

"Right."

He hung up and saw his mother in the kitchen, motioning him to her.

"Yes, Mom?" he said.

She pointed at a double-layered chocolate cake on the table.

"Take this to the Kantellas," she said warmly. "And tell Paula to come over sometime. We have missed her."

Joey realized that Paula hadn't been over since Mary had the skiing accident. That really must've bothered her.

He smiled. "It's a pleasure, Mom," he said.

4

THE FIRST TUESDAY of July was turning into a hot, humid day even before the sun had started its climb into the blue, almost cloudless sky.

Joey's first thought was of the lake, and he went outside before breakfast to get a close look at it. It was smooth as china as far as he could see, and dark blue as it reflected the sky. Seagulls flew above it in wide circles as if in time to a music heard only by their own ears. A quintet of ducks glided at a V-shaped angle low over the water, almost touching it. Far on the other side of the lake a boat was droning along like a bee.

"Oh, wow!" Joey cried happily.

He ran back to the house and gulped down his breakfast.

"Did you see that lake?" he asked cheerily. "It's like glass!"

"Perfect for that swim," remarked Yolanda, dishing up two of the jam-filled Hungarian pancakes on a plate for herself.

"Yes, if I were ready. But I'm not," said Joey. "I've got to put in some long swims first. Five miles. Ten. It's a great day to try it."

"Not right away, though," advised his mother. "Wait two or three hours."

Joey smiled. "An hour to an hour and a half is soon enough. Mom."

He excused himself and left the table. He began to mosey toward the kitchen, paused with his hand on the doorknob, and looked at his sister.

"Got something on for today, sis?" he asked.

She looked over her shoulder at him with a mischievous twinkle in her eyes. "Yes. A big movie star is picking me up at nine."

"Yeah, sure. And he's going to have you costar with him in his new movie."

Yolanda laughed. "Okay. Why do you want to know if I've got something on today?"

"I'd like you to go alongside of me in the boat," he said. "Will you?"

"Sure. Why not? Dad say we can take the boat?"

Joey nodded. "Yes. He said it's okay."

At ten o'clock Joey made his first attempt at swimming across the lake, a distance of two and three-quarter miles. He began with a moderate, steady pace, swimming freestyle, left arm up and over, then down into the water to sweep him forward, repeating the procedure with his right arm, while he kicked slowly and steadily with his feet. His breathing was smooth, even.

The yards flowed under him . . . twenty-five . . . fifty . . . seventy-five. Now and then he looked at the opposite shore. Was he really closing the gap? he wondered. It hardly seemed so.

Eventually Yolanda, who was in the boat with Mary, said to him, "Joey, we're about halfway across."

The news startled him, made him feel good. He swam on, the muscles in his shoulders, thighs, and legs beginning to give signs of pain. But light pain, hardly enough to complain about.

At last he was within thirty feet of the opposite shore. He looked up and saw a gleam of pride in his sisters' eyes.

"You've swum two and three-quarter miles,"

Yolanda informed him. "How about that? How do you feel?"

"Great."

"Okay. Let's turn and go back."

He turned and headed back, maintaining the same rhythm, and just a slower pace. On and on . . . stroke, stroke, breathe . . . stroke, stroke, breathe. Little by little the muscles in his body began to protest more, and he began to wonder if he'd be able to make it back. Two and three-quarter miles each way added up to five and a half miles. If he made it, it would be quite a feat.

At the midway point he took a brief rest, then swam on. He was within a mile from his home shore when he began to feel a faint, nauseous sensation in his stomach. He tried to ignore it, as he tried to ignore the little stabs of pain in the various parts of his body.

On and on he swam, his arms getting heavier with each stroke so that his elbows barely moved out of the water now. The smooth, steady rhythm was gone out of his kicks.

"Keep going, Joey," Yolanda said to him. "You've only got a little way yet."

The aches got worse. The nauseating sensation spread.

"Just a little way more, Joey," Yolanda's voice

encouraged him. "About another hundred feet."

On and on . . .

Then cheers and applause went up from the small gallery of spectators as he came in close to shore. His head began to swim. The nausea was about to explode.

He knew the territory now, so he stood and began to walk the remaining fifty feet or so to shore when he felt it coming up. He stopped and threw up on the water, washed the vomit away, and threw up again.

Then he stood there, breathing tiredly, until he was sure nothing more was coming up, and walked weakly up on shore.

The cheers and applause had stopped. His mother ran up to him, an anxious look on her face. "Joey!" she cried, grabbing him by an arm. "Do you still feel like vomiting?"

"No. I feel better, Mom," he said. "I just want to sit down."

He started for the deck near the shanty and saw Gabor and Paula, and a man who looked vaguely familiar, quickly coming toward him. Yolanda and Mary were docking the boat.

The man put an arm around Joey's waist and helped him to the deck.

"Here. Rest yourself," he said. "You'll be okay."

Suddenly Joey remembered where he had seen the sun-bleached hair, the tanned face, and the rugged physique before. The man was Sam Harvey, Merton High's swimming coach.

Obviously Paula had told him about Joey's wanting to swim the lake. Did he come to give me pointers? Joey wondered.

"Good swim, Joey," Paula said, beaming at him. "You did stop on the other side, didn't you?"

"No."

She stared at him, surprised. "You didn't?"

"No," Mary piped up. She and Yolanda had docked the boat and had come to join the small crowd. "He just turned around and swam back. And you know what? He swam almost as fast coming back as he did going across."

"Marvelous!"

Joey tried to hide his embarrassment over Paula's outcry. Anyone might think he had just done the impossible.

"Joey, this is Coach Sam Harvey," Paula said, after her initial excitement had died down. "He's swimming coach at Merton High."

"Yes, I remember seeing him at the meet," said Joey. "Hi, Coach. I'm glad to meet you."

"I'm glad to meet you, too, Joey," said the coach as they shook hands. "Congratulations.

That was a good swim. Especially since you didn't stop for a rest on the other side."

"Thank you."

"What did you have to eat before you started, by the way?"

Joey thought a minute.

"I baked for you *palacsinta*," his mother reminded him, smiling. "Don't you remember?"

"Oh, that's right," he said. "That's something like pancakes, Coach Harvey. This is my mother."

They exchanged greetings and shook hands. "That might be why you got sick, Joey," said the coach. "Those pancakes could be very tasty, but you'd better lay off them before a long swim."

"I thought it wouldn't hurt if you got some pointers from a real professional," Paula cut in, her eyes intently on his.

Joey smiled. "I guess I can use all the pointers I can get," he said.

"From what you've just demonstrated, I think you've already learned a lot of them," said Coach Harvey.

"Thank you, sir."

"You exercise every day?"

"Yes, I do. I use barbells, and do isometrics and isotonic exercises, too."

The coach grinned amiably. "Fine. Was this

the first time you've swum across the lake and back?"

"Yes."

"Start from the south end the next time. Swim about seven miles and increase that by about a couple of miles each day. Watch for cramps. Do you know what to do in case you're caught with one in a calf, for example?"

"Pull up on my toes and massage the calf at the same time," replied Joey, remembering what he had read about half cramps and other cramps that afflicted the various muscles in the legs, ankles, and arches.

"Sounds like you've done your homework, young fella," observed Coach Harvey, smiling.

"A lot of it, anyway," said Joey.

"You know about the rest periods? They're most important on long swims. Take them, whether you think you need them or not. They'll relax your muscles, keep them from getting cramps, and keep you from getting tired too quickly."

"He rested only once coming back," said Mary.

"I really wasn't that tired," confessed Joey.

"There's the point," said Coach Harvey. "Don't wait for the tiredness, or the fatigue, to hit you first. Rest, swim a distance, rest again.

You don't have to rest very long. Thirty seconds is enough." He looked at Joey's arms, shoulders, waist, thighs, and legs. "You've really built yourself up a strong, terrific body, son. Know what? I wish I had you on my swim team. I think you've got the makings of a champion."

Joey smiled modestly. That was the greatest compliment ever paid him. "Thanks, sir," he said. "Thanks very much."

"Save it until you've finished that swim," said the coach. "Taking any vitamins?"

"No."

"Start taking vitamins C and B, about two tablets of each a day, after meals. Lake water tends to be cold most of the time, and one thing swimmers must guard against is colds. Vitamin C will help keep colds away. Vitamin B helps in various areas, especially against headaches and indigestion that can happen after spending a lot of time in the water."

"That's good to know," said Joey, deeply appreciative of the coach's help. If he had come across anything about vitamins in the books he had read, he couldn't remember it.

"But, getting down to the nitty-gritty," said the coach, "probably the two most important things to know about, and put into your daily routine, are exercise and diet. Include orange juice for breakfast, but lay off anything that'll lay solid in your stomach, like pancakes. Save that *palacsinta* for the evening meal." He smiled. "Cereal is good. Orange juice again for lunch, with meat, vegetables, and fruit. Meat again for the evening meal — for its protein, you know — with salad, peas, and beans."

He paused, and looked at Joey with an amused glint in his gray eyes. "You know, even the most famous swimmers got to the point when they hated to train. But it's that self-discipline and drive that puts the men above the boys, Joey. You train right, and you'll find that your goal will be easier to get to than you think."

"Thanks, Coach," said Joey.

5

IT WASN'T until eight days later that he was able to try another long swim in the lake. Bad weather — it either rained hard or the water was too rough — had been against him.

That morning, just before ten, he followed Coach Harvey's suggestion and rode to the south end of the lake in the boat to begin his swim from there. Yolanda and Paula accompanied him. During the ride, Paula explained why she had brought Coach Harvey to meet him that day over a week ago. Neither one had seen each other since then.

"I met him during the Saturday morning swim meets," she said. "Ross introduced me to him."

"I figured that," he said.

She smiled. "Look, we're just good friends, Ross and I. His parents and mine have known each other for years. His father and mine work at the same place. They're both engineers. They come over to our place, my parents go to theirs."

"You go with them?"

"Sometimes. While our parents play cards and have a few drinks, Ross and I listen to records."

"Must be fun."

"Oh — it's okay."

"I bet," he said.

He stopped the boat about fifty feet from the farthest end of the lake, keeping away from the sea weeds that were choking up that area.

"Okay, take over, Yo," he said to his sister. A moment later, he dove into the water. It was cold, but it always felt worse when he first entered. After a few minutes, as he started to take long, powerful strokes through the water, his body became acclimated to the temperature, and soon he thought no more of it.

He saw Yolanda pulling the boat up to his left side and slightly behind him, and there she maintained it at a slow, steady speed.

Thoughts of the talk with Coach Sam Harvey went again through his mind. He had started to follow part of the coach's recommendations the very next morning when he had added the vitamins to his breakfast and resisted the tempting rolls of *palacsintas* that had been left from the day before. Why did Mom always have to make so many that there had to be leftovers? Even *they* were delicious!

Sometime later he took a brief rest — about thirty seconds — then went on.

"We've just come opposite the red barn on the hill," said Yolanda after a while.

"Okay!" he acknowledged.

The red barn. He and his father had drawn a map and clocked the distances between various landmarks a few days ago. The red barn was exactly three and a half miles from the south end of the lake.

He swam on, still feeling no aches or pains, not even a tiredness creeping into his bones.

"We're opposite the gabled house," advised Yolanda.

Five and a half miles. Moving along — slowly, surely.

After a half-hour more in the water, his legs and arms were getting to feel like lead. There were muscles in his shoulders that were beginning to cry out with pain — muscles he hadn't known he had. His chest was beginning to tell him things, too. Put them altogether, and he got the all too inevitable answer: he was near the stopping point.

How far had he swum? How many miles? What was the next landmark? Right now he was so tired he couldn't remember where it was.

"Okay!" he cried, his arms and legs unable to function another second. "I'm stopping! Right here!"

Yolanda quickly pulled the boat up beside him and reversed the engine to bring the craft to practically a dead stop. Joey grabbed the aluminum ladder that hung over the side, then took Paula's extended hand and climbed aboard.

"Man, I'm tired," he said, collapsing into a seat in the stern.

"You shouldn't tire yourself so, you dummy," scolded Paula. "What do you want to do — hurt yourself and *not* be able to make that long swim?"

His chest rose and fell as he inhaled and exhaled heavily. He closed his eyes and felt his head spinning.

I hope I don't get sick, he thought.

He didn't.

He opened his eyes and looked at the sprawling hill of brown and green fields to his right.

"Where are we?" he asked. "Did I pass another landmark?"

Yolanda glanced up from the sheet of paper she was holding.

"Twin white silos," she said. "Where are they?"

"There!" Paula pointed ahead. "Up there next to those trees!"

Joey saw them and tried to remember what the distance was from the south end of the lake to the silos. Before his memory could focus on the mileage, Yolanda exclaimed proudly, "Ten miles! You've almost swum ten miles, brother!"

Joey couldn't believe it. Yet there was the proof. The silos.

"More like nine," he said. "I'd have to go another mile before I'd be opposite those silos."

"So what's another mile?" said Paula, smiling. "So you've swum nine! That's not bad, man!"

Joey grinned, pride dancing in his eyes. "No, I guess it isn't. That's not bad at all."

Four days later, on a Friday almost as calm a day as last Tuesday, he swam to a point just beyond another landmark, a white stone building visible for miles. It was fifteen miles, and it was late afternoon when a cramp in the calf of his left leg forced him to stop. It felt like the jab of a sharp instrument, and he started to do as he had learned if that situation arose. He pulled up on his toes with one hand and rubbed his calf vigorously with the other. The cramp disappeared, but he was tired all over. Every muscle in his body seemed to ache, as if each of them had gone beyond the straining point.

But reaching the fifteen-mile landmark wasn't bad. It was a six-mile gain over the other day.

How many guys had ever swum fifteen miles? He was sure that Ross Cato hadn't. But Ross was a sprinter, a short-distance swimmer. It wouldn't be fair to compare Ross with himself.

He was making progress on the goal he had set out for himself. That's all he wanted: to conquer the whole twenty-one mile lake at one shot. Suddenly he'd be famous. Sixteen-Year-Old Kid Swims Twenty-one-Mile-Long Oshawna Lake. His picture would be in the papers. Maybe the feat would even attract national attention. Maybe TV cameras would be there when he walked up on shore at the end of his swim, and the next morning his celebrated swim would be described on the "Today Show" and the "Good Morning Show." Maybe he'd even be asked to appear in person on one of the shows. Look at Steve Cauthen, the jockey who was only eighteen when he rode a triple-crown winner. Look at all the national publicity he collected.

Television would be the best exposure, because people could see how small he was and how remarkably great he was in spite of his stature.

His family would be proud of him. Especially his father, who was a small guy, too, and had had his nose rubbed into crud by his tall, fat-bellied boss because of it. His father hadn't quit his job yet, but that was because he hadn't been able to find another one that paid more, or even as much. The way inflation had risen, he couldn't afford to get another job at a cut in pay.

Joey knew that his parents were putting a little money into a savings account every week, but he didn't know how much. He didn't care. The money was earmarked for a college education for each of the kids, and the occasional out-of-state trip for his mother and father.

Then came a day in August when he felt as if he suddenly were two separate persons. A part of him wanted to go swimming, the other part didn't. The part that didn't — won.

It was an ideal day for swimming, too; the water temperature was about seventy-five degrees. But the desire seemed to have been drained out of him.

"What's the matter?" Yolanda asked, surprised. She was already in her swimsuit, and Mary and Gabor were in theirs, too, ready to plunge in. But Joey had made no move to change.

He shrugged. "I don't know. I just don't care about going in today," he said.

His sisters stared at him as if they couldn't believe their ears.

"It's perfect weather for it," said Mary. "And the water's great. You sick or something?"

"No. I feel okay. I just don't want to go in. I want a break. I think I'll take in a ball game for a change. I haven't seen a baseball game all summer. Okay?"

Yolanda shrugged. "Sure. That's okay."

Mary nodded. "Yeah. That's okay."

"See you all later," he said.

He thought he sounded a little bitter. But maybe they hadn't noticed it. He couldn't explain what had come over him. He just didn't care about going swimming today. That was it. Period.

He ran all the way to the ball park some two miles away and sat through nine innings of a game that had both exciting and dull moments. It was between the Lions Blue Sox and the Moose Barons. The Lions won, five to one. By the time he got back home he was ready for dinner, just as if he had burned up a lot of energy and it needed replenishment.

He didn't go swimming the next day either, or the next. And each day he didn't go made the thought of swimming less and less desirable. He had never dreamed that he would see the day when swimming would get to him, but that's what had happened.

He cut down on his exercises, too. But not much. He enjoyed fooling with the barbells. He could exercise with them anytime, day or night, and they kept him in shape.

But swim the twenty-one-mile long Oshawna Lake? He had second thoughts about it now. Now, the year he had planned to swim it, he was having second thoughts!

It was the continuous grind that had gotten to him. The grueling daily exercises. The almost daily swims, even if they were only during the summer.

The rewards? What rewards?

Maybe the feat would creat a lot of excitement for a while. But once that excitement died down, who would remember the swim except him and his family? Eventually his family, too, would forget it. Only he would remember it.

Heck, he had a right to change his mind, didn't he? It was his mind. He was older now. He knew better.

Twenty-one miles. *Crazy*.

Aunt Liza was outwardly pleased when one day in early September Yolanda told her that Joey had second thoughts now about swimming Oshawna Lake.

"Second thoughts?" she echoed. "You mean he has changed his mind?"

"I think so, Aunt Liza."

"Is that right, Joey? You are not going to swim the lake?"

He was watching an old John Wayne movie on television. He didn't want to go into a lot of explanation about what had gone on in his mind, because he was a little confused about what he really intended to do in the future, anyway. But he had to be honest with her, so he said, "I don't know for sure, Aunt Liza. But it isn't because I'm afraid to try it. It isn't that."

"No matter what it is, Joey, I'm just glad you are not going to swim it. Twenty-one-miles! *Isten!* Only a crazy person would want to swim a lake that long!"

"That's what I've begun to think, too, Aunt Liza," he confessed.

"If you're not afraid to try it," Yolanda cut in, "what is your reason for quitting?"

He didn't like the word *quitting*. He didn't like the sound of it. It was like calling him a coward, and he was no coward.

"I got tired of it," he said irritably. "I got to thinking that I've wasted two full summers doing nothing else but exercising and swimming. I'm not getting ready for the Olympics, you know."

"I thought that swimming the length of Oshawna Lake was almost like that for you," said Yolanda, her voice noticeably quieter.

"Maybe it was, at first. But no more. It's nothing. It's just a big, long lake sitting there. It's been there for thousands of years, and it'll be there for thousands more. Not me. I'll be here for a short while, then pssssst! I'll be gone. So who'd give a good darn if I swam it, or if anybody else swam it?"

"But you had a reason to swim it," she said firmly.

"Not anymore."

"You wanted to prove to people —"

"Not anymore."

"And to yourself —"

"Cool it, Yo," he snapped. "I don't want

to prove anything anymore to anybody."

"You've chickened out."

"Yo!" he cried, staring at her.

"Okay," she said, raising her hands, palms outward. "Okay. I won't say another word."

THE THIRD YEAR

1

HARDLY ANYTHING more was said by any body in the family — including Aunt Liza — during the late fall and winter about Joey's change in attitude concerning his swimming the length of Oshawna Lake. There were plenty of things going on at school that kept him occupied — football, wrestling matches, basketball — sports he didn't participate in but attended competitions. But he roller skated when there were roller-skating parties, joined the chess club, and became an avid reader of war stories.

He kept exercising because it gave him one thing he was especially proud of: a well-developed, healthy body. He'd like to keep it that way if he could without working his tail off as he had done during the previous two years.

The new school had been finished late in the summer, in time for the students to start in the fall. It was a big, sprawling, red-brick structure that covered acres of land. It had a new football field and around it a track where meets with the various schools in the district were to be held. There were also a new baseball diamond and a tennis court. All it seemed to lack in the way of sports facilities was a swimming pool.

Joey's father was still working at the same old place and still griping about his foreman. He hadn't looked for another job during the winter. Most of the time the weather was too lousy to drive to work in, let alone drive around seeking a new job. He hadn't given up, though. He had promised his wife that much. He'd be damned if he'd spend the rest of his life working for that fat-bellied so-and-so. The word he used in Hungarian was funnier, Joey thought, than the English equivalent he used sometimes.

Joey went out for track and was encouraged by the track coach, Bill Harris, to concentrate on sprints. When the first competition came around in April, he entered the one-hundred and two-twenty yarders and came out third in both.

Meanwhile he kept running three miles each

day, except Saturday and Sunday, and one day Coach Harris pulled him aside and said he'd like Joey to run the mile and the two miles at their next meet.

Joey agreed. On the day of the meet, he entered the mile and two-mile events and came out first in both.

His picture was in the *Gatewood Courier* the following day, with an article about him accompanying it.

> Little Joey Vass, participating for the first time on Gatewood High's track team, has proven to many experts that size and stature are no detriments when it comes to running track meets.
>
> This is his first year on Coach Bill Harris's team, and although he came in third in the one-hundred and two-twenty yard meets, his performance in the mile and two-mile events deserves praise. He won both events, the first time that a single runner from Gatewood has ever done so in its track history.
>
> It seems that Little Joey Vass has found his niche.

There it was, thought Joey. 'Little Joey Vass.' The allusion to his size again. Would it ever end? Perhaps not. It had never ended for his father; it might never end for him, either.

Paula called him on the telephone that same evening that his picture and the article appeared in the paper.

"Hey, man, you're a celebrity!" she said. "Beautiful!"

"Thanks, Paula."

"I didn't know you liked track."

"Well, I had never thought about it. Not until this year, anyway."

"I hope it's not going to stop you from swimming altogether."

"It won't."

She knew. She had known about it since last fall. Yolanda had told her after Paula had wondered why she hadn't seen Joey in the water much anymore, even on some of those hot days in the fall.

"Okay. See you at school, Joey," she said.

"Thanks for calling."

On Sunday afternoon, he got a phone call that hardly went on for three seconds before he recognized the speaker's voice. It belonged to Ross Cato.

"Hi, Peewee. How you doing?"

"Okay. What are you doing here? Aren't you in college?"

"Yes. But my father had a stroke, so I came home for a few days."

"Sorry to hear that," said Joey.

"Thanks. But he'll be okay. Hey, great publicity you raked up, man. Nice going. But you sure surprised me."

"Why?"

"I didn't know you were in track."

"This is my first year," explained Joey.

"So I read. And doing darn well in it, too. Hey, this is *the* year, isn't it?"

Joey frowned at the wall picture he was looking at. "*The* year?"

"Yes. The year of the long swim."

He didn't know, Joey thought. No one, not even Paula, had told him that he had changed his mind about swimming the lake.

"Oh," said Joey. He made a sound like a laugh.

"You haven't chickened out, have you?"

"Me?" That stupid sound came out of his mouth again. "Well —"

"Well what?"

"Just well, that's all."

Ross laughed.

"You mean you're thinking of forgetting the

whole thing? Hey, man, you're not worried that a small guy might not be able to make it, are you? I heard you were a regular pint-sized dynamo."

Joey's hand tightened on the receiver. He hadn't thought about the swim for weeks. He didn't believe Ross was still teasing him because he was short.

"Size has nothing to do with it," he said, his throat tightening.

"Don't tell me you really have chickened out," said Ross. "Why don't you admit it? You know what? I suspected all along that you would."

Joey squirmed. He felt sweat come to the palm of his hand, sticking it to the receiver.

"I've got to go, Ross," he said, feeling himself losing control.

"Hey, Joey, wait a minute."

Sweat beaded his upper lip, tickled it, and he wiped it off.

"Yeah?"

"Look, I'm sorry. Don't get mad. I didn't mean to insult you. Really, I think what you've already done took a lot of guts."

Joey frowned. "What do you mean?"

"Paula told me about those practice swims you made last summer. Five miles, seven, even up to fifteen miles. Just doing that should be a feather in your cap."

Is he pulling my leg, or is he serious? Joey wondered.

"Thanks, Ross," he said.

"Take care."

"You too."

He heard the phone hang up on the other end, and hung up, too.

You've chickened out, Ross's words echoed in his mind. *Why don't you admit it?*

Joey closed his fists and cursed Ross up and down for talking to him like that.

The hell with you, Ross! he said bitterly to himself. The hell with you!

2

THAT VERY NEXT EVENING he began to get serious about training again, multiplying the time he had spent on the back press, the half-knee bends, the sit-ups, the leg stretching exercises, because he had cut down on them all. It was May, and the water was still too cold to go in swimming, so he jogged on the road, running two miles one way, two miles back. The next day he would increase the distance to three miles one way, three miles back.

He worked on the bench in his room, lying on it and taking long, freestyle strokes as he would do were he swimming in the water.

His family became aware that he was back into full training again, and let him go without trying to discourage him. They hadn't tried to before; they weren't going to now.

As a matter of fact, his sisters and brother seemed more enthusiastic about his ambition now than they were before. Gabor would come into his room and watch him exercise, something that previously seemed to have no appeal to him whatever. Now the kid, ten years old on his last birthday, had become so interested he began to do the same exercises Joey did, though for fewer repetitions.

"I thought sure you had given up the idea of swimming the lake for good," Yolanda said to him one day. "You seemed very depressed."

"I guess I was," he admitted.

"What made you change your mind?"

He thought for a moment.

"That handsome Adonis, Ross Cato," he confessed.

"Him? How could he —?" She was staring at him, wide-eyed.

Joey grinned. "It's hard to believe, isn't it? But I owe my change of mind to him, my nemesis."

"Nemesis?" She looked at him puzzledly.

"Oh, never mind," he said.

She smiled. "I think I know. Paula. Right?"

He shrugged.

"She have something to do with your change of mind, too?"

"No. It's just what he had said to me over the phone one day. He said he knew I would chicken out."

"Strong words. So that's why you've changed your mind. He challenged you."

He nodded. "Yes. But not only him, either. I've reconsidered my values. I'm going to do it for the same reason I had planned on doing it in the first place."

"You're going to prove you can perform a feat that a lot of guys in this world can't."

"Not only guys," he corrected. "Girls, too. After all, a woman swam across the English Channel. Maybe someday a woman will swim the twenty-one miles of Oshawna Lake."

"Maybe it'll be me," she said, and smiled. "In a pig's eye! I wouldn't even swim *across* the lake."

"Why not?"

"I have no desire to. It's not my worldly ambition."

"What is, Yo?" he asked her. "What is your worldly ambition?"

They never had talked about ambitions before. Hers or his.

She lifted her shoulders, swung around so that

123

her dress spiraled around her legs, "Teach music. Getting married. Having a couple of kids. Preferably one of each."

"Nothing wrong with that," he said, and suddenly imagined two tiny tots running around, shouting at him, "Hey, Uncle Joey! Look!"

"Yeah, that'll be fun," he said, smiling.

That Friday evening Joey's father said that he was planning on going fishing the next morning if the weather was fair.

"Want to go with me, Joey?" he asked.

"I will, Dad!" Gabor piped up fervently.

"I asked Joey," said his father.

"Sure, Dad," replied Joey. "I'll go. I haven't been fishing for a long time, anyway."

His father smiled. "You sure you can break away from your training for a few hours?"

Joey smiled back. "I'm sure."

They got up at six A.M. the next morning. The sky was clear and the lake smooth. They packed their tackle and rods into the boat and took off, both trolling at a slow speed as they headed south on the lake.

"So you have changed your mind," said his father, fixing his blue eyes on Joey.

"About swimming the lake? Yes."

"Why? Because you are still hurt that some

people call you Peewee and such names as that?"

Joey thought carefully before he answered. "A little bit, Dad, but that really doesn't bother me half as much anymore as it used to. I think it's boiled down to two things: I made a promise to swim it, so I want to keep that promise. Number two, I want to satisfy myself that I can do it."

"Good," said his father. "I'm glad. You know, I would not tell you this before, but when I found out that you had decided not to swim the lake, I was disappointed. I thought that here is my son — no bigger than a pea, like his father — training every day, working his hind end off to prove to the world he can do something very few other people can. Then, all of a sudden, I see you would not go through with it. I was surprised, because I was sure you were very determined to do it. In bed your mother and I would talk about you swimming the lake. You think we did not think much about it? Oh, yes! We both were afraid for you, but she especially. Your mother is a very sensitive woman. She loves you children so much she worries her head off when any one of you gets just a scratch. Can you imagine what she thought when she heard you wanted to swim the lake? The long way yet? The whole twenty-one miles of it?

"But we talked about it and talked about it, and I told her I know how you must feel. Being smaller than most other boys your age is tough. When I was a young boy, my friends called me *madár*. You know what that means?"

"Bird," said Joey.

"Yes. Bird. In a play our class put on in school, I was the Baby Jesus because I was the smallest one in it."

"In a play in the first grade I was the Littlest Angel," said Joey.

"Yes, I remember that." His father laughed, and happy tears blurred his eyes. "But is it different today? No! I am Little Napoleon! Little La Guardia! Little this! Little that!" He shrugged. "But what the hell. I laugh it off. These men who call me such names do it because they like me. I know that. We are good friends, everyone of us. All but that s.o.b., my boss. He is the one who takes the advantage. He is the only one of them all who can call me a bird and make me feel like a cockroach. Someday . . ." He shook his head sadly. "Oh, I don't know. I want to find another job, but it is hard. Very hard."

"Well, he's got to retire someday, Dad," said Joey. "Or maybe he'll die first."

"I might die before he does," replied his father, smiling to make a light joke of it.

"No, you won't," said Joey. "You're too good to die early. There are too many of us who love you. We want to see you grow real old."

His father put an arm around his shoulders, leaned forward, and kissed him. When he leaned back to straighten up in his seat, Joey saw tears in his eyes again.

"I love every one of you, too, Joey," he said, his voice almost breaking as he spoke. "You are all good children. And you are right. I don't want to die right away. I want to see you all grow up, and be healthy and happy. That is what your mother and I want to see."

Joey nodded, and they settled back into silence as they waited for the fish to bite. As the sun warmed the air, Joey leaned back and relaxed. He'd remember this morning for a long time.

3

ON MEMORIAL DAY Joey swam across the lake and back. The water was about sixty-eight degrees, warmer than usual at this time of year because the weather had been exceptionally warm.

"How do you feel?" Yolanda asked him as he stood in knee-high water and waded to shore. She had ridden the boat alongside him during his swim, taking Mary and Gabor with her.

"Okay," said Joey. "But I hit some real cold spots out there."

"It's too early for a swim like that," said Mary. "It's better to wait until next month."

"That starts day after tomorrow," reminded Gabor.

They laughed.

Joey went to the house and found, to his dismay, that Aunt Liza was there. She was clutching her purse as if she might be leaving soon.

"Are you swimming today?" she said, staring at him as if he had lost his mind. "Joey! The water must be like ice!"

"Almost, but not quite, Aunt Liza," he said, giving her a smile as he went past her, water dripping from his trunks.

"I shall never understand your letting him go swimming like that, Margaret," she said, addressing her sister-in-law. "Never."

"He's not a child, Liza," said Joey's mother calmly. "And he's a good swimmer. Very good."

Joey's smile lingered as he headed for the bathroom to shower and change.

The news that Joey was going to swim the length of Oshawna Lake spread through the school. Kids took bets on him. Most of them were against his succeeding. They ranged from two to one to ten to one, with five to one the most common.

"You got to make it for me, Joey, ol' boy," said one of the guys who had made a bet that he'd succeed.

"You quit before the twenty-one and I'll dunk you," warned another, jesting.

Joey promised them not to worry. What other promise could he dare make?

He met Paula in the hall on his way to Chemistry II.

"Hi, Paula."

"Hi, Joey! Are *you* popular! Hear the bets being made on you?"

"Crazy," he said.

"I think it's cool," she said. "I've got a bet on you, myself. I'm betting five to two that you'll do it."

"Five dollars?" He stared at her incredulously.

"No. A dollar and a quarter to fifty cents. Big gambler, aren't I?"

He grinned. "Safe, anyway," he said, feeling better. "I hope Mr. Thomas doesn't hear about this. He'll want to confiscate the winnings."

"He'll have to wait until fall," she said, her eyes laughing. "By the way, can I ride in the boat with Yolanda when you make your next long practice swim?" she asked hopefully.

"Of course. But I don't think that'll be until next month. The water's quite cold yet."

"Will you let me know?"

"Sure."

"Thanks, Joey. Oh, I think it's so *exciting*," she said, squeezing up her shoulders.

They were at the doorway of the Chemistry II classroom. Joey opened it and followed her in.

Exciting? I don't know, he thought. I had never realized it was going to create such repercussions. If I had ever dreamed that there would be bets on me swimming the lake . . . I don't know.

It was a good thing he enjoyed chemistry. There was enough going on throughout the entire class to keep his mind off swimming for at least one period during the day.

When exam time came, he passed them all, though just squeezing by in ancient history. He just couldn't care about the collapse of the Roman Empire or the cradle of civilization.

The next Saturday, a hot, muggy day that sent the thermometers shooting up into the high eighties, was the best yet for a swim in the lake. Sticking to his promise, Joey called Paula and said he was going to try a long swim at about two in the afternoon — maybe ten miles.

Okay, she said. She'd be over about five to.

She was, and the three of them — neither

Mary nor Gabor cared about going with them this time — rode the powerboat down to the south end of the lake.

"It's such a gorgeous day, I'd be tempted to shoot for the twenty-one," said Paula, gazing at Joey through her dark sunglasses.

"I've thought of it," said Joey. "But I'm not ready for it. I've got to get in the mood."

"In the mood?" Paula echoed. "Suppose we had another hot day like this — we're bound to, you know — and you *didn't* get in the mood?"

"I'll be in the mood when I make up my mind to be," promised Joey, putting one leg over the side of the boat. "Anyway, I'll start in the morning. I figure on swimming it in about fifteen hours — approximately."

He dove in.

The water was cool. But Joey's body temperature soon adjusted to the water, and he became comfortable with it as he began his long, freestyle strokes.

The yards went by. Eventually a quarter of a mile . . . a half-mile . . . a mile passed by. He felt good. The smooth surface of the water made the swim easier, too.

He didn't know how much time had gone by when he suddenly heard Yolanda's voice: "Two miles."

Good, he thought.

Sometime later he heard it again: "Five miles, Joey."

He swam on, taking his time, not pushing himself, resting a few seconds, resuming the swim.

He went by the seven-and-a-half-mile landmark and thought he heard a distant rumbling. He glanced up at the sky and saw the normal array of white clouds he had seen earlier. Their shapes had changed, of course, but they seemed to be moving more noticeably now, and it made him suddenly aware that the surface of the lake was no longer smooth as it had been when he had started his swim. It was getting rough. Damn! he thought.

He saw the sky brighten up briefly as a flash of lightning split the sky behind him. Thunder rolled like distant drums.

"Joey," said Yolanda. "I think you'd better call it quits."

"The storm's coming this way from the south," observed Paula.

He looked behind him without losing a stroke and saw the darkening clouds merging into one another, twisting, curling, leashing into each other as if they were strange, wild animals of another kingdom. Again a flash of lightning lit up the sky, and thunder boomed.

"Joey!" cried Yolanda. "Come on! It's dangerous being out here with that storm coming toward us!"

Damn the storm! he thought disgustedly. Why couldn't it have held off for another few hours?

He turned and headed for the boat, grabbing the ladder as the craft started to go slowly by him.

Paula smiled at him. "You swam about eight miles," she said. "How do you feel?"

"Good," he said, taking a deep breath as he relaxed on a seat.

"Thirsty?" She began reaching for the gallon thermos filled with cold lemonade.

"Yeah. I'll have a glass of it," he said.

She poured him a glass, and he drank it down slowly.

"Hey, I felt some drops," she said, and turned to look at the blackening southern sky. "Oh, man, look. I bet it's pouring down there."

"Goose it, Yo," said Joey. "I don't mind getting swamped; we've got swimsuits on. But I don't like that lightning."

She shoved the throttle as far forward as it would go, and the boat responded, its bow cutting through the waves like a knife blade through butter. The rain began to pelt them before they got the boat to shore on its sheltered hoist. Soon they were running to the deck below the steps. They stopped and let the rain drench them as they watched the swiftly approaching clouds and the display of lightning that streaked across the sky.

"You know what that's going to do?" Joey said, gazing with despair at the white-capped waves.

"What?" asked Paula.

"Cool the water back to what it was in May."

"Why are you griping?" said his sister. "Old man sun will come through. He hasn't failed us yet, has he?"

He didn't find her remark funny. "Come on," he said. "Let's go up to the house."

4

IT WAS a perfect Thursday morning in late July when Joey started the long trained-for twenty-one-mile swim. He had gone to bed early the night before and had a good night's sleep. In the morning he had a light breakfast of orange juice, cereal, and milk and was in the water at exactly five minutes after six.

Accompanying him in the powerboat were Yolanda and Paula. Both of them had brought their cameras and enough orange juice, water, and food to keep the three of them supplied for a full day.

None of them had told anyone else — except members of their own families — that he was going to start the swim this morning. It wasn't until two days ago, anyway, that Joey had decided that this morning would be the day. He had been keeping an ear close to the weather reports, and that good man, the meteorologist, had promised ideal weather for the next twenty-four hours. It could change abruptly, of course; sometimes it did. But in this case Joey felt that he had to accept the forecast as final.

The morning couldn't be clearer. There were hardly any clouds in the sky. The air was still, the lake calm. Sea gulls glided around in wide circles overhead. Some sat on the water, ruffling their wings and bathing. The water temperature was seventy-eight. Joey couldn't ask for anything better.

A mile . . . two miles . . . and then five finally lay behind him.

Joey took his time, gliding through the water smoothly, left arm up, over, back, right arm stretching forward, then down, fingers close together, pressing down into the water, sweeping him forward. He lifted his head just enough to breathe at every stroke of his left arm. He had found breathing easier this way. It was less tiresome, more comfortable than taking two or more strokes before he breathed. Left arm stroke

— breathe. Right arm stroke, left arm stroke — breathe. He rested a while. Swam on.

"It's noon," Yolanda said, breaking into his quiet thoughts. "Want something to eat?"

"Okay," he said, and treaded water while he partook of a small glass jar of beef stew. He finished it, handed the empty jar to his sister, drank a few ounces of milk, rested a while longer, then swam on.

The midday sun shone on his back and arms and danced off the water that splashed from his hands as he lifted them in a smooth, steady rhythm, first one and then the other. One . . . two . . . one . . . two . . .

"We're opposite the Girl Scout Camp," announced Yolanda a short time after he'd eaten lunch.

He didn't bother to look, but he knew the landmark. A large, rust-colored building some sixty feet from shore. A playground was in front of it. Small, rustic cabins set in the woods beyond it.

He had swum eleven miles or thereabouts.

Only ten more to go. Oh, man.

He swam on, and little by little he began to feel the telltale messages of pain in his arms, his shoulders, his thighs, and his calves. He tried to ignore them, knowing that thinking about them might only begin to disillusion him. He forced himself to think of other things — of home, of his family, of Paula.

Paula.

Would she go out with him? he wondered. Would she like to be my girl? Does she have any idea how I feel about her?

Now and then the aches interfered with his thoughts, and tiredness began to take a firmer hold of him.

Hunger finally gnawed at his stomach again, and he was glad when he heard Yolanda say, "It's six o'clock, Joey. Want something to eat?"

Six o'clock. He'd been swimming almost exactly twelve hours.

"You kidding?" he said, stopping to tread water. "I'm starving!"

This time he ate two small glass jars of peas and tunafish, a bar of candy, drank a glass of milk, and got going again.

Later, he saw the sun beginning to lower over the western hills, the clouds in front of it looking like stretched sugar candy.

He began to glance now and then at the shore some two hundred yards to his right, at the high cliffs that separated the lower areas where cottages and all-season homes stood only a few feet above the lake's edge. Steps led in some cases from a boat dock to a home up on the plateau.

When he saw the one with a wide platform midway up he knew where he was, and from a previous calculation determined that he had gone about eighteen miles.

"Yo!" he cried, enthusiastically. "Only three more to go!"

Both girls looked wide-eyed at him.

"How do you know?" his sister asked.

"Those steps," he said. "The one with the wide platform halfway up."

They looked at the landscape. "I see it," Paula said.

"I do, too," replied Yolanda.

The boat was slightly behind him and to his left side, at a distance that had hardly varied since they had started.

"How do you feel?" Paula wanted to know.

"Tired!"

"Hang in there," she said.

The water was still calm. It seemed even calmer now than it was during the midday hours. The weather and the water couldn't be better.

The sun had dropped behind the hill, leaving a dazzling, flaming orange sky, when Joey felt a stabbing pain in the arch of his right leg.

"Oh, no!" he yelled, stopping and letting his legs go limp.

Yolanda stopped the boat. "What happened?" she asked, staring at him. Paula rose off her seat, her eyes wide as she stared at him too.

"I've got a cramp in my arch!"

"A cramp? What luck!" His sister looked beyond the bow of the boat, at the point of their destination. *Joey's* destination. He followed her gaze, and saw the familiar peak-roofed pavilion of the park just beyond the beach.

How much farther did he have to go? he wondered. A mile? A mile and a half?

"Can you do something about it?" Yolanda shouted to him.

"I'm going to try!"

He reached down and grasped the arch of his right leg as hard as he could. With his other hand he grabbed his toes and pulled up on them. When he started to sink below the surface of the water he let go of his leg, pushed himself back up, and filled his lungs with air. Again he clutched the arch of his leg and pulled up on his toes. After doing it four or five times he tested the arch.

"It's gone!" he cried happily. "The cramp's gone!"

The girls let out a cheer, and Paula got back behind the wheel of the boat.

"Ready to swim on?" she asked.

"Ready!" answered Joey.

He resumed his swim: left arm up and over, right arm pushing downward, closed hand propelling him forward. Right arm up and over, left arm pushing downward; left arm reaching up and over, feet kicking.

On and on and on.

His shoulders ached. His arms and legs felt like leaden weights. He had slowed down considerably.

"Keep going, Joey!" Yolanda encouraged him. "Keep going, brother!"

The orange sky had darkened. Night was falling fast.

A boat came shooting through the water toward him, its bow light piercing the growing darkness. Then another came, and another. They swept around in wide circles and took places on either side of Joey and the girls' boat. The occupants waved and smiled and gave the "V for victory" sign.

"How about that?" said Yolanda, returning the wave and the smile. "An escort!"

Photographers were snapping pictures. One boat carried a man with a TV camera. He aimed it at Joey, kept it on him — swung it toward the girls for a few seconds, then back on Joey.

Oh, Lord, how much farther? thought Joey.

His arms were like sticks ready to break off. His neck, shoulders, thighs, and legs ached. He wouldn't make it. It was impossible. He had gone his limit. He had to stop. He just had to.

"How — how much farther?" he called out.

"Not much, Joey!" his sister's voice came to him. "Hang in there a little longer. Just hang in there, brother!"

"I can't!"

"You've got to, Joey. You've got to. Just a little longer."

He swam on — tiredly. Oh, so tiredly.

Then, at last —

"Joey! You did it!" he heard his sister shout. "You did it! You swam the twenty-one miles!"

He looked up at her. She was standing in the boat, her arms extending into the air, her face beaming with joy.

"You did it, Joey!" she cried again, and jumped into the water beside him, splashing him with it. He stood then, finding the water only up to his chest. Then Paula jumped in, too, and both girls swung their arms around him and kissed him.

Tears stung his eyes. His heart pounded from

tiredness and fatigue, but also with joy. He wanted to shout out to the world, to yell at the top of his voice and let everyone know how thrilled and happy he was.

I did it! I swam Oshawna Lake! Do you hear me, everybody? I swam Oshawna Lake!

Cheers sprang from the crowd standing on the sandy beach. Many of them — men, women, teenagers — waded into the water, their clothes on, shook his hand, and offered their congratulations. It was a sight he had never expected to see in his life.

They've come to see me, he thought. Me!

"You son-of-a-gun," said a familiar voice. "You did it! You actually did it! Congratulations, Joey!"

Joey smiled. "Thanks, Ross," he said. They shook hands.

He could barely make it to shore, but with Paula and Yolanda on each side of him, he managed. He was met by the rest of his family — his mother, father, Mary, and Gabor, and even Aunt Liza, who gave him a hard, wet kiss on his cheek.

"Crazy boy!" she said, looking at him with happy, tear-filled eyes. "But look what you have done! Everybody in town has come out to see you! You have become a big person! A very big person!"

"She is right, Joey," smiled his father affectionately. "You have become a very big person. Everyone will soon know of Joey Vass, the boy who swam Oshawna Lake."

"Excuse me, Mr. Vass," a woman interrupted, holding a microphone in one hand and a tape recorder in the other. A Press button was pinned to her lapel. "That was a remarkable feat you've accomplished."

"Thank you."

"Did you ever feel like stopping? Did you have any problems during the twenty-one mile swim?"

"No. Excuse me. I'm tired. I want to get home and go to sleep." He started to go past her.

"Did you ever feel that you might not make it, Mr. Vass?" she asked, following alongside him.

"Just . . . toward the last," he said.

"Nothing you'd like to add?"

"Nothing."

"Are you glad you made the long swim? Do you really feel that you have made a name for yourself in the field of swimming?"

"I don't know about that," replied Joey. "But, yes, I'm glad I made the long swim." He saw Yolanda and Paula looking at him, their faces wreathed with smiles. A memory, almost like a dream now, flashed through his mind.

"Yes," he went on. "If I don't ever do anything else like this again, I'm glad I made that swim. It was an experience that I — and my sister and my friend, Paula Kantella — will never forget."

"Thank you, Mr. Vass," she said, pleasantly.

There was that man again with his TV camera focused on him, and other photographers were taking still pictures of him. But he didn't care about any of this, now. He was tired. He wanted to go home and sleep . . . and sleep.